I0661745

Charles Grissen

Ideala

A Romance of Idealism

Charles Grissen

Ideala
A Romance of Idealism

ISBN/EAN: 9783337346744

Printed in Europe, USA, Canada, Australia, Japan

Cover: Foto ©Andreas Hilbeck / pixelio.de

More available books at **www.hansebooks.com**

BY

CHARLES GRISSEN.

THE TRADE SUPPLIED BY

THE SAN FRANCISCO NEWS COMPANY, 210 Post Street
San Francisco, California, and
THE J. K. GILL COMPANY, Portland, Oregon.

TO

LOUIS MADDOCK, M. D.,

THIS ROMANCE IS INSCRIBED

BY HIS FRIEND,

CHARLES GRISSEN.

IDEALA;

A ROMANCE OF IDEALISM.

PREFACE.

Being past that period of life when youthful ardor and mistaken ambition might lead one into temptation to appear in print, one is prepared to take in full measure all the blame and adverse criticism without apology; safe, inasmuch as matters personal are concerned, which are no part of the story nor of the public. Suffice it to say that, whilst the author believes in the cultivation of our highest moral and intellectual faculties, he believes no less in doing our duty in the every-day, common affairs of life : for, whatsoever one's duty and work may be, "Act well thy part, therein all the honor lies." Hence ours is a double duty; the one to society, the other obedience to the promptings of our inner nature ; and if performed in the spirit as expressed by Seneca : " There is not any man, either so great or so little, but is yet capable of giving and receiving benefits."

CONTENTS.

IDEALA.

IDEALA.*

INTRODUCTION.

On fancy's pinions rise with me
Beyond the far off southern sea ;
Unto the wind your wings expand,
Above the sea, above the land !
Æolus, king of upper air,
Will bid Boreas guide you there,
Across earth's rugged central line,
Beyond the southmost cape's confine ;
Beyond the deep, mysterious sea—
The dreamland of sweet poesy.
In happy visions there behold
A brighter life to you unfold.
Let loose the strings of memory then,
And dream dear fancy's dreams again :—
As once you dreamed those phantasies,
Those sweet and castled vagaries
Of high ambition's vaulted towers,
Of Love's enchanted rosy bowers,
Beneath an azure sky serene,

---

* For the sake of euphony and rhythm Ideala should
  be pronounced Ideälä.

INTRODUCTION.

Beneath Hope's bright and golden sheen ;
While tender thoughts like music roll
In soothing tones athwart the soul ;
Hushing in sweet forgetfulness
Life's daily burdens, pain, and stress.
Aye, dream again those golden dreams,
While yet the fitful beacon gleams
From off life's fast receding shore.
Fair Faith, bright Hope, come, higher soar !
In fancy free arise with me
Unto that isle beyond the sea,
Fair Eidolon, the Isle of Peace,
The isle beyond the southern seas !

There lives in every human heart
A longing for a better part ;
To rise above conditions base,
Above our narrow circle's gaze—
But, like a shipwreck lost at sea,
The soul as helpless seems to be.
Life's fullest measure has its grief,
The strongest faith its unbelief ;
Affection sweet ofttimes grows cold,
And friendship, held at par with gold.
We look on high—we look beyond—
We hope for something more beyond
The silent sea—a better life
Than blasted hopes and ceaseless strife !
Then follow me beyond the sea—

Brave toilers, toil on patiently ;
From morn till night, from day to day,
Wherever duty leads the way.
The patient heart and hopeful soul
Betime shall reach life's fondest goal,
While yet, along the darksome way,
The brightest star—Hope—sends a ray.
Then follow me beyond the sea,
Brave toilers.   Toil on patiently ;
To you I sing my song, to you !
To every patient toiler who
Would follow me beyond the seas,
To Ëidolon, the Isle of Peace,
Sweet isle beyond the southern seas.

CANTO I

I.

The day star in his fading glory,
Lay panting on the evening sky,
His hot breath steaming high above him,
Dissolved the gold of upper air,
Until the earth and all the heavens
And all the vast unfathomed deep
Below him, as a sea of fire,
Seemed glowing, burning, ruddy red.
Like forkéd tongues, that, leaping, flaring,
From out the pent up fires arise
Against the russet sky, thus glistened
The distant mountains' snowy peaks,
Like beacons placed in semi-circle
Upon the island north and east.
And far below, primeval forests
Rose darkly 'gainst the purple sky :
Low brooding vapors hung above them
Augmented by the curling smoke,
That slowly in dun wreaths ascending,
From humble homes in forest glades,
Gave the gray mists still darker shades.

II.

Within the realm of this deep forest,
All life that late was animate
With lusty vigor, seems suspended.
The golden glory above the pall
Of crouching vapors, did not enter,
Nor penetrate the sylvan shade,
Save where, perchance, the shifting shadows
A vacuum left, through which poured down
A flood of golden light, that, streaming
Upon the leafy canopy,
Fell through the tangled mass of foliage
Upon the quiet world below,
As rays through iridescent windows
Invade a temple's holy shade.

III.

No breeze plays through the leafy branches,
The strings of Nature's harp are mute ;
And silent are all the musicians
Whose countless voices shook the wold.
The chattering apes cease their grimaces,
And look with stupid wonder down
From their high seats among the branches
Of the banyan and the tamarind.
Around a fan palm tall and slender,
A reptile winds its plated coils ;
Another glides with lazy motion,
Past where a sable antelope

In dreamy, guileless mood is standing
Unmindful of the reptile's fangs.
Within her lair of ferns and grasses,
Where the sweet-blossomed nilho grows,
The brindled lioness caresses
With tender look her playful cubs.
Beneath a cluster of tall tallipots,
(Whose queenly flowers beautiful
Bring death unto the tree that bears it,)
With royal mien the monarch stands,
The bravest of the forest's creatures,
Now like a proud but gentle king.
Secluded in his lair lies stretching
His glossy limbs the spotted 'pard ;
His eyes have lost their baleful lightning,
And all his sinews are unstrung.
Even the tiger's fierce, wild passions,
Seem at this hour all subdued ;
As 'neath the cassia's scented blossoms,
He strides about with harmless step.
The wings of all the birds are folded,
And hushed are all their varied songs ;
Save where, perchance, some hungry stripling
Expands his beak with piping sound.
The savage beasts and creeping reptiles,
And all the feathery tribes alike,
Their hunger and their passions sated,
On Nature's bosom seem to rest.
Peace reigns throughout the island forest,

Transcendent calm and restful peace ;
While from the breath of myriad blossoms,
From flowers pregnant with perfume,
The breezes waft the sweetest odors
Far out unto the dreamful sea.

IV.

Along the forest's edge, a river
Flows tranquilly towards the sea ;
His shining face bedecked with blossoms
And leaves that fall perpetually
From countless boughs and fragrant flowers,
The sport of zephyr and of stream.
A strangely fashioned boat glides slowly
Adown the broad and tranquil stream,
Propelled by many strong-armed oarsmen,
Towards a city fair to view.
Of timbers light the boat is fashioned,
In shape like some huge water-fowl ;
The sides in graceful curves expanding,
The prow, high arched, like neck of swan.
Inside and out, securely fastened
By skillful hands, the boat is lined
With skins, well oiled, from brutes ferocious,
Whose hides once served their purpose well,
But serve their purpose now still better
As hides impervious to the flood.
On either side, strong arms are plying
Four oars, with steady, measured strokes ;

Thus like a swan, with wings expanded,
With stately motion glides the boat,
With its light load of boughs and arbors,
Down o'er the slow and shining stream.
Dark skinned, of olive hue, the oarsmen
Are tall in stature, and their hair,
Of inky blackness, falls in tresses
Down o'er their shoulders broad and strong.
Their bearded faces and their bearing
No low nor menial race betray.
Their clothes alike, a simple garment,
Of grayish cloth and texture fine,
Around the waist with belt is girdled,
Leaving quite bare their sinewy limbs.
There is among this crew another,
Of whiter skin and smaller form,
And clothes made of a different pattern,
A little man of foreign race,
And Maripo by name they call him.
Beneath the boat's high prow sits he,
With book in hand, absorbed in reading
A chapter from King Solomon.
He reads aloud his favorite chapter,
And ever faster move his lips,
Till with the light of inspiration
His small black eyes are all aglow ;
All else around him seemed oblivion
As deeper in his theme he plunged.
The crew did seeming take no notice

Of the strange action of this man,
But talked among themselves, discussing
The features of the morrow's feast.
The forest's shadows now grew deeper
Upon the river's shining flood,
As lightly o'er the waters glided
The boat upon its downward course;
Until the forest lay behind them,
And wider grew the shores apart;
Here fertile fields and groves and meadows
On either side expanding lay,
From whose sweet breath the evening breezes
Their perfume bore toward the sea.
"Husta!" exclaimed the stalwart oarsmen,
Rowing with energy renewed,
As in the last rays of the sunset,
Locked in a crescent bay secure,
Before them lay the shining city
And towers of fair Ammiel.*
But downward still the boat goes gliding;
Now past some groves of richest fruit,
And gardens of voluptuous verdure,
Surrounding, hiding in their midst
The bamboo cots of lowly dwellers.
But none of these sees Maripo;
For to himself he still sits reading
A chapter from King Solomon.

---

* Capital of Eidolon.

The shores on either side now rising,
As swiftly onward sweeps the boat,
With every stroke seems growing higher
Into great cliffs precipitous,
Which in a rock-ribbed gateway ending,
Stand high above the city's walls.
Past these, with slower strokes are rowing,
The boatmen to their landing place,
Where flow the waters of the river
Into a smooth and placid bay.
The boat is moored, the oarsmen leaving,
Allow a throng of willing hands
To carry off the boughs and arbors,
Designed to grace the coming feast.
A load upon his shoulders bearing,
With lively step goes Maripo
Unto the house of Rhoda Mahib,
Mahib, the ruler of the isle ;
And there, before the portal, greeting,
Stands Blos O'Hare, the Irish maid.
" Ah, Mademoiselle, to you good even,"
The little Frenchman spoke, low bowing.

CANTO II.

NIGHT IN THE PALACE.

I.

Night, on her soft wings descending,
Reigned o'er the island city, and
With wand more powerful than Ceres',
Brought all the world beneath her spell.
Wane Sorrow from each heart departing,
And Pain, her pale-faced sister, soothed,
And Envy too, and Hatred, leaving
Reluctantly the hearts they swayed,
The stately Queen of night obeying;
All fled from her like fleeting clouds,
Save Love alone, serenely smiling,
With rapture kissed the starry queen.
Within the palace, drowsy stillness
Pervades the high-arched lofty halls.
Hushed are the songs of exultation
That late did ring through hall and court;
And in his starlit lonely chamber
There meditating sits the chief.
"O Night, fair queen, with joy I hail thee!
Oh, let me drink thy magic balm!
For thy sweet moments of oblivion,

Thy visions, dreams, and phantasies,
Thy stillness and thy peace transcendant,
Are Hope's bright sunshine to my soul.
Thy presence brings me loved communion
From the unfathomed mystic shores ;
Thy voices coming ever nearer
As slowly sets life's trembling star.
This truth I learn upon reflection :
As comes and goes the changeful moon,
Men come and go, and are forgotten ;
And honors—baubles of a day—
But fill the heart with empty longing,
Still leaving men unsatisfied.
Though twice have I been chosen ruler,
Of all the people of Eidolon,
And but to-day, the greatest honors
Have they bestowed upon my head ;
Yet, here to-night, I'm glum and lonely
Within these walls that are so mute !
Ah, one sweet voice I love is dearer
Than all the shouts of vain applause.
And what of honor and ambition
To one true and devoted heart !
Before the altar of affection,
All men alike obeisance own.''
Thus to himself spoke Rhoda Mahib,
Absorbed in meditation deep.

II.

By many high-arched walls divided,
In her apartment sat alone
Good Blos O'Hare, sat there a-napping,
To cheat the hours' weary flight,
While waiting for her lady's coming,
From Shala's* sacred walls.

　　　　"Wake up!"
Thus voices spoke, "O sleeping maiden,
And show thy blooming face to us;
The moon is risen high in heaven,
And all the stars attend her flight!"
Thus from her slumber was awakened
Miss Blos O'Hare by servants rude,
Whose clamor she did put to question
For cause of this undue alarm.
In answer, Maripo, low bowing:
"Ah, Mademoiselle, I beg—I beg—
Your pardon, Mlle. Blos—good even;
Behold, my love—thou art so fair!"
Then Blos O'Hare spoke, interrupting:
"An' what is it yer a jabberin' now?"
"I hear the voice of my beloved ——"
"Oi hear, an' what d'ye mean disturbin'
The pace o' night wid all sich talk?"
"Ah Mlle., what I've been a speaking,"
Humbly continued Maripo,

---

*Native temple dedicated to the worship of the sun, and pre-
side l over by a maiden priestess

" Is speech that I have learned in reading
A chapter from King Solomon."
" An' ye're a Dave, i' faith ye are."
Replied Miss Hare in angry tones.
" Oh ! be not angry with your brother—
O sister with the shining face—
O sister with the hair of fire !
Your brother with the lotus* face,
He who doth love the withered flower,†
And talks to it caressingly,
As women talk and laugh to children."
A servant thus to Blos O'Hare
In his own native tongue addressed her.
" O sister he's a noble fellow !"
Came from the lips of still another.
" O sister, hear thy brother speak !"
Remarked a third one of the servants.
" Ah, Mlle Blos," spoke Maripo,
Still bowing low, " my master sent me
With greetings to your lady ; he
Did send me at this hour to tell you
Of my great love to you—said he :
' Thus tell the lady's maid, To-morrow
I'll meet her at the outer gate,
Before I speak to her great sire.' "
" An' be me soul, what be yer meanin',
Ye are a pair, ye and yer master ;

*White face.
†Maripo's Bible.

He mait me at the outer gate,
An' send his greetings to me lady—
An' ye to spake of love to me—
An' he to spake to my great sire,
Who (bless his soul) is dead an' gone.
Hark ye, Oi hear me lady's comin'! "
Sweet voices singing now are heard,
Distinctly coming nearer and nearer ;
As from the temple on their way,
The virgins come with Mahib's daughter.

III.

"An' sure, me lady, bless yer soul,
A long time is it Oi've been waitin';
Oi've been a-workin' very hard
To get all ready for the morrow—
An' sich a splendid, glorious robe ! "
" My dearest Shining Face," in answer
The Mahib's daughter, to her maid ;
" But of my father tell me, woman,
Is he not waiting for me ready ?
To his apartments now conduct me,
O daughter with the shining face."
In whispers to her lady speaking,
Miss Blos remarked with serious air :
" That Frenchman Coquin sent his greetings
To you, me lady, by his servant,
By Maripo, just now he sent them."
" And is this all the message he

Did send by Maripo his servant?"
" An' sure, me lady, he did spake
Some stuff about King Solomon."
"Aye, it is well; now thou may'st leave me,
For here my father he is coming."

IV.

" Ah, daughter, long have I been waiting
Thy coming from the holy place ;
And if I not misjudge my vision,
Thou art with cares oppressed, my child."
In answer thus the Mahib's daughter :
" And truly, father, dost thou see :
But if with care I be afflicted,
It is for thee, my father dear.
Thy brow betrays increasing cares,
No more with mirth thy eyes are beaming,
And scarce are seen thy lips to smile :
Though all the people pay thee homage,
They love thee not as well as I.
Oh, I could chide these very people
For robbing me a father's care,
And thee of rest so well deserving.
To know thee great, my inward pride
Is touched with pity and compassion,
When fame demands such sacrifice,
And public honor such conditions."
Her father thus in answer spoke :
" My child, I well perceive thy meaning,

And prize thy kindly heart far more
Than all the honors of my station.
But life has duties, yes, and many,
To which all men own strict obedience ;
First to our loved ones and our homes,
Then to the state and to the people.
My child, I have not been neglectful
Of duty which is due to thee ;
And as to duty due my people,
I do that every man should do.
But list, my child, I must be speaking
Of some affair which is thine own,
Which more than else has been oppressing
My mind and heart with cloudy cares—
Art still resolved and firm in purpose,
To take the vow of Virgin Queen ?
Which, if I be not misconstruing
The signs presaging such events,
Thou wilt be chosen queen to-morrow. '
Be well assured, my child, I would
Not lead thee from a righteous pathway,
Nor cross thy purpose well directed ;
But hasty youth will make resolves
That end more often in repentence.
Bethink thee of the rigid vow,
The obligation, cares, and burdens ;
To take all these upon thyself—
A child, from childhood just emerging !
Bethink thee well, my child, of this.''

The Mahib's daughter thus made answer:
"My father, thou hast wisely spoken,
I think no less than thou hast said,
Nor should you think less of my motion,
That serving but my purpose in
What thou callst duty due the people.
Where childhood ends, there should begin
A life of useful thought and action.
O father! cease thy cares for me:
Accept my prayers and my good wishes,
Wherefore I ask thine in return."
With reverend salaam she departed,
To leave her father to his thoughts:
While she her own apartments seeking
Called for her maid, the Shining Face.
But Blos O'Hare heard no one calling,
Being engaged in argument
With Maripo, who came returning
In haste, demanding to be heard:
"O Mlle. Blossom! please you listen
To something I forgot to tell you,
When I this evening called to see,
Sweet Mlle. Blossom—oh *ma chere!*
It is of you I heard him talking."
"An' who'd yer hear a-talkin' o' me?"
"My master, love, my master, he——"
"An sure your master sir's a villain—
What did he say? Why don't ye spake!"
"Ah, Mlle. Blossom, please you listen:

My master's not a villain—he
Did say, the people had decided
To make me darling virgin queen.
Whatever that does mean precisely
I know not, but, by Solomon,
I fear, my love, it is disgraceful
To be a queen of virgins here!"
" Yer master is a rogue. I tell ye ;
An' be swate Mary, ye may tell him,
I niver was no queen, nor virgin,
An' niver 'spect shall aither be."
Then to the chamber of her mistress
Turned Blos O'Hare with hasty step.
But here her service was not needed ;
For, wrapped in sweetest slumber, lay
The Mahib's fair and only daughter.
" An' bless me soul, she is a-sleepin,"
Soliloquized Miss Blos O'Hare.
" An' she's as pretty as a picture,
The darlin' child, God bless her soul.
An sure, Oi would not now be livin'
(It breaks me heart), but for this child :
To think, so far away from Erin,
An, niver, niver more go back !
Och, it's so sad—good night, me child."
Then to her couch herself retiring,
In sleep's embrace soon were forgotten
The tears of good Miss Blos O'Hare.
Within the palace of the Mahib,

No sound disturbed the restful night ;
Peace reigned supreme beneath the penon
Of that hushed night on isle and sea.

CANTO III.

From out the depths of ocean darted
Great fiery arrows to the skies;
Before them mists and vapors parted,
And sped away as by surprise.
While, in a beauteous roseate light,
The Orient heavens grew expanding,
Till earth and sea and sky were blending
In russet splendor—wondrous sight!
Then on his golden chariot rising,
Swift rolling, came the lord of day;
And all the isle with life rejoicing
Seemed thrilled beneath his potent sway.
The shining orb is now arisen,
The ghostly vapors sped away,
And Night, which held the isle in prison,
Dissolved before the light of day.

I.

Behold fair Ammiel stands attired
In garlands for this festal day!
Above the flower-wreathéd pillars,
Above the high-arched gates and from
Each house, the flags and pennants floated.

The roads were strewn with scented boughs,
And banks of fragrant flowers skirted
The fruitful lawns on either side :
And stately palms, broad-leaved, imparted
Their cooling shade along the roads.
Like some fair garden in the springtime,
The breath of fragrance filled the air ;
And birds from every bush were singing
Their morning carols sweet and clear.
Large-eyed gazelles were quietly browsing,
And peacocks proudly paced the lawns ;
And birds of rainbow-wing were fluttering
Among the palms and blossoming trees.
From bloom to bloom the sun birds darted,
And mottled parrots vainly swung
From fruit to fruit ; while agile monkeys
Searched chatt'ring for their morning meal.
By two broad avenues divided,
The roads between the ancient dwellings
In perfect circles winding lay.
Beginning in the centre, where,
Within the city's inner circle,
The palace of the Mahib and
The spacious halls of state were standing,
Surrounded by sweet-scented groves
And lawns and gardens, where fresh fountains
Their silvery streams upsending, fell
In dancing sprays of rainbow colors,
Into their cooling beds below :

Between these and nearest dwellings,
Like Saturn's shining rings, there lay
A broad and open space, where started
The two broad avenues, out-spreading
In opposite directions straight.
To ocean's sandy beach one leading,
And one unto a rocky bluff,
Whereon the pride of Éidolon,
The lofty temple Shalah stood.
From palace, circle after circle,
In perfect order winding lay,
Each growing wider than the other
Unto the very uttermost.
One row of houses, lawns, and gardens,
Between two roads smooth built of stone ;
In ever varying beauty changing
One circle from the other, yet
In harmony the whole expanded
Into a city wondrous fair.
The houses all one story high,
Were built to shelter many people.
The walls like alabaster shone,
With surface polished smooth as mirrors,
Relieved by pannels of stucco-work
And frescoes of symbolic patterns.
Beneath the ample cornices
With many quaint and curious carvings,
There birds had built their little homes.
Thus row on row, amidst the foliage,

The beauteous dwellings seemed alike :
But high above the city tow'ring,
The lofty hall of state arose,
Enclosed by wings in semi-circle,
With marble pillars studded 'round,
The terraced front to northward looking,
Contained a court with marble paved.
To southward joined the Mahib's palace,
Its graceful arches tow'ring high
Above the city's comely dwellings.
But high above the hall of state,
The rounded dome of beaten copper
Shone as a cresset in the sun,
Its burnished surface flaming, gleaming
O'er all the island far and nigh.

II.

The sun had journeyed full four hours
On his celestial voyage, when
The people of the island city,
In simple festive garments clad,
Their daily cares and work abandoned,
Were gathered on the streets and lawns.
Full many were in groups assembled ;
Grave men, with weight of years, beside
The matron, youth, and bright-eyed maiden,
In pleasant talk, or list'ning to
Some words of council that were spoken :
In manners gentle and refined ;

All seeming of one rank and station ;
All by one central purpose moved.—
A sudden sound, like thunder rolling,
Now broke upon the multitude,
Like trumpet blast among the soldiers ;
All seemed to know the signal call ;
To right, to left, in perfect order,
Some here, some there, their places found.
The roads that late were filled with people,
Are free and clear for passage now ;
The women to one side retiring,
Unto the other all the men.

III.

Lord Coquin on his coal black steed,
By Maripo alone attended,
Threw rein before the palace gate.
With lordly air he looked about him,
At the unusual wond'ring throng,
His eager eyes for some one searching.
Yet finding not the object sought.
" Ah there, monsieur, I see her coming ! "
Spoke Maripo to Lord Coquin ;
As with an air of much importance,
Towards the gate came Blos O'Hare ;
Who, when he saw her, all indignant,
Lord Coquin turned to Maripo.
" Me lord, good mornin', bless yer honors,
Oi'm here mesilf, why did ye want

To mait me at the gate sich toime, sir,
I' faith, a bit o' toime Oi hive,
Me lady now is at the temple—
Oi niver seen the loike o' this—
An' sich a robe for Queen o' Virgin !"
Quite calmly Lord Coquin replied :
"Go tell the Mahib I would see him
Upon some matter of import ;
With haste return and give his answer
For which I shall be waiting here."
Past all amendment was this plunder,
But Lord Coquin expedients knew.
With message came Miss Blos returning :
"An' sure, me lord, the Mahib said
He would be pleased instant to see ye."
Leaving his steed with Maripo,
Lord Coquin strode toward the palace ;
Passed servants and passed gaping crowds,
Passed groups of elders and dignitaries,
And maids attired in festal robes,
And tripping children scat'ring flowers :
From hall to hall, onward he strode
Straight to the Mahib's audience chamber.
A goodly number of the elders
And of the chiefs were there assembled.
Lord Coquin made a salaam grave
Before the ruler and the elders,
Then of the Mahib asked permission
With him in private to confer,

Which granted, Lord Coquin proceeded :—
"Great Mahib, Chief of Ëidolon !
Thou hast to me been friend and brother ;
A stranger I, cast on thy shores,
In gratitude I'm bound forever,
My noble lord, to thee.
           'Tis true,
Though poor I be, through adverse fortune,
Yet am I not a menial born ;
But far away amongst my people,
Was I a chief, e'en as thyself :
'Tis therefore, my presumption pardon,
For I would speak of some affair
Pertaining to thy heart and station.
Thou hast, my lord, an only child,
The fairest 'mid the island's daughters,
And if I err not in my judgment,
My lord, your daughter will be chosen
Virgin Queen to-day.
           Tell me,
Is it her wish, or thine, I pray thee,
To offer this great sacrifice ;
Depriving you of her sweet presence,
And placing on her shoulders fair
The cares and burdens of an office
That may prove fatal to your child,
The sweet and lovely Ideala ?"
In answer thus the Mahib spoke :
"My brother from the far off islands,

What thou hast spoke is very truth ;
And grieved am I to lose my daughter,
But her resolve is firm and strong,
And none may change her from her purpose.
Though we owe duties to ourselves,
Yet must we serve the state and people ;
My daughter's heart obedience knows—
But hark ! e'en now the drums are calling,
With deep and mighty voice, the start
For all the people to the temple—
The consequence be left with fate—
I thank thee, brother, for thy council,
Now to the temple let us hence.''

IV.

While yet the rosy lips of morn
Kissed every flowret's pearly cheek ;
While yet the breath of zephyr wafted
Its perfume over hill and plain,
Unto the monarchs, hoary-headed,*
From whose high crowns, the golden light
In radiating shafts descending
On Shalah's† temple slanting fell,—
A group of virgins were assembled
From every island district three,
In numbers full three score or more,
All robed alike in purest white,

---

* Snow-capped mountains.
† Native name for temple of Virgin Queen.

Save that a scarf of different shading
The districts of the maids distinguished.
Their busy fingers shaped sweet flowers
In garlands for the temple walls ;
While rang the music of their voices
In laughter and in converse sweet,
And now and then some roguish damsel
Exchanged her work for play and dance.
Now round the temple slowly pacing,
The merry maids this song did sing :—

Hail !   Hail !
The Spirit of Fire, the great rises higher,
        In triumph he is come !

Hail !   Hail !
From Shalah's great spire, his arrows of fire
        Rekindle the world !

Sing, sing,
The praise of the beautiful, modest and dutiful
        Sherezad* our queen.

Sweet, sweet,
Is the life of the flowers, blossoming flowers,
        The children of Om !†

Sweet, sweet,
Is the life of the gold-winged, fluttering dream-winged
        Butterfly gay !

Sweet, sweet;
Is the life of the singing, the ever light winging
        Birds of the air !

---

* Name of present Virgin Queen serving in the temple.
† Om, name of Deity—Oriental.

Sweet, sweet,
Is life, when its measure is innocent pleasure
To sorrow unknown !

Fleet, fleet,
Is life, as the fleeting, quickly retreating
Clouds of the sky !

Sing, sing,
While youth is expanding, her golden wings lending
A dreamy ideal !

Sing, sing,
Ere sorrow is growing, and tears are flowing,
And the heart be as stone !

Sing, sing,
For the seasons are going, the seasons are wooing
Us all to the grave !

The signal from the great drums rolling,
Like thunder fell upon their ears.
From out the dark-eyed circle steping.
Two modest maidens now advanced :
A flow'ry canopy each mounted,
One to the right, one to the left
Of Shalah's proud and lofty portal.
Upon the right a maiden sat,
In grace and beauty all surpassing,
In face and form a very queen.
Her dark hair fell in wavy tresses
O'er neck and bust of perfect mould :
Her large dark eyes a soul revealing
Serene and pure as seraphim,

And lips, whereon love found expression
Mid blush tints on her olive cheeks.
A snow-white garment from her shoulders
And from her thighs in ample folds
Down to her tap'ring feet extended,
A wreath of dewy flowers crowning
Her shapely head and queenly brow,
The symbol of virginity.
Such was the Mahib's only daughter,
The sweet and lovely Ideala.
Upon the left sat Arrah's daughter,
A rival worthy of the fairest
In bearing, form and face and mien ;
The lovely huntress, sweet Diana,
Might not unenvied her behold,
Auma, beloved of all the people,
For gentleness and kindly deeds.
These were the virgin candidates
High seated on their festive thrones :
While round them stood attendant maids
With tablets to record the vote.

V.

From every circling street came pouring
Into the long, broad avenues,
The people led by chiefs and elders
Towards the temple of Shalah.
The chiefs on handsome horses riding,
A guard formed round the virgins' thrones ;

The multitude in order passing,
With banners and with spears they came
Before the virgin candidates,
And with salute made known their choice.
When shadows fell no longer slanting,
Then from the drums the signal came,
Announcing that the vote was over,
And that forthwith all should repair
(Except the Mahib, chiefs, and elders)
Towards the ocean's sandy beach.

VI.

Here was the scene of sport and pleasure,
Here every annual festal day:
Here youth and strength did match each other
At varied games and feats of arms.
The throng with much impatience waited
The chiefs and elders to appear.—
" Hark ye ! hark ye !" the heralds shouted,
" Hark ye. O people of Éidolon !
The vote is taken and decided,
And ere the lord of day sinks down
Beyond yon deep, mysterious sea,
Then in her temple reigns your Queen,
The Mahib's daughter, Ideala."
Then rose from the assembled hosts
Tumultuous shouts of approbation ;
But when old Ageram was seen
Upon the high arena standing,

His flowing locks white with the frost
Of many years about him streaming,
His arms extended high as if
To bless the multitude beneath him ;
While round him in strange contrast stood
The temple maidens young and fair,
Their new elected Queen surrounding
(Who like a very goddess seemed,
Upon her throne the fairest maid).
Now was the storm of voices calmed,
And Ageram, the island's prophet,
With solemn voice thus spoke :
                          "O sacred sun !
O light celestial in the heavens !
O lamp eternal, giving light
And life to all the living creatures !
Thee we behold in splendor rise
From out the ocean, never failing,
And mark with reverent eyes thy course,
Until thou fadest from the heavens
Into the gulf of night beyond.
Ye see, his sacred rays are falling
Upon the temple of Shalah ;
Oh, praise him all ye island people !
He blesseth now our Virgin Queen
Elected priestess in thy temple.—
Behold a sign, portentious omen !
The great one hides his fiery face
Behind a cloudy veil—this moment—

Some evil may befall our Queen—
Some ill may to the people happen—
For thus the augurs spoke of old,
And I, your Ageram, have spoken."

CANTO IV.

THE RACES—THE STORM—ARRIVAL OF THE STRANGER.

I.

" Now are the judges all appointed.
Of whom the Mahib chief presides,
Who will, in fairness and in justice,
Decide the contests of the day ;
None will be honored undeserving :
And each shall have an equal chance
To match his skill and prowess fairly
And win distinction if he can.
Let none with rankling heart retire,
Nor envy in his bosom hide ;
For honor lies not in the hamstring,
Nor virtue in the strength of fist.
Then forth all youths who seek promotion,
Who would from parent guardianship
Advance unto the rank and station
Of Atma,* novice of the state.
By fours in numbers be ye starting,
Unto you goal assigned for ye,
While ten times ten the strokes are counted

---

* A secondary, or preparatory rank to citizenship.

Upon the drums, in measured time."
Thus spoke Arrah, the chief, addressing
The youths now ready for the race.
Full many a score of youths impatient,
With eyes aglow and beating hearts,
The signal from the drums awaited.
The start was made, and how they flew
Along the sandy beach, swift·footed;
Chest close to chest, the head poised high,
Each aimed to reach the goal a winner.
Yet many were those left behind ;
To them another chance was given,
A test of strength and skill upon
The pliant bow, to send unerring
An arrow to its distant mark.
Then called Arrah upon some others,
Who had in previous years obtained
The rank of Atma, yet would enter
Into the rank of Astaba.*
Then from the throng at once came forward,
And forming into ranks they stood,
A splendid troop of manly youths.
A sword and spear to each was given,
Which he who won might then retain.
Through all the varied exercises
Arrah himself commanded them.
They won applause and admiration,
Of all who saw their skillful feats.

---

* The rank of full and free citizenship.

And now the contest for the prizes;
Throwing the spear unerringly
Some forty yards while swiftly running.
Few were the winners in this feat,
And proudly they received the honors,
The highest rank of Astaba
Bestowed on them with great distinction.

II.

The games suspended for a time,
The people sought for other pleasures.
In groups some stood, commenting on
The games and contests that were over ;
Some talked of Shalah's new-made queen ;
While others sought the bath refreshing
Among the ocean's cooling waves.
Some from the venders bought refreshments
Of choicest fruit and meat and cake ;
And over all the children's voices
In merry laughing rounds were heard.

III.

" Behold, behold ! " an hundred voices,
With one accord cried out aloud.
" Behold, the angels of the darkness
Appear upon the field serene,
Dread heralds of the stormy regions,
Oh, see them rising from the sea !
In serried massive ranks advancing,

With blackness of the night they come !
Oh, Arrah, haste and call the races,
Ere the dark legions dim the light
Of day, and drive with madding fury
The foaming waves upon the shore ! ''
Arrah to southward gazed intently,
With ;troubled look upon his brow ;
Yet calmly called he for the races,
The last great contest of the day. '
He called upon the youths to enter,
Those who would yet high honors win ;
Those who had failed in contests previous
To win the rank of Astaba.
Then shouts of glad anticipation
Escaped from many a youthful breast,
And from the throng a glad approval,
Like echoes rolling ran along.
Nor had their voices ceased, when other
Shrill, screeching sounds were heard afar,
With every moment coming nearer,
And growing louder, shriller still,
And more distinct and more discordant.
O'er the fair sky a massive wall
Of dreadful blackness now expanding
Rose from the sea towards the isle.
"Orkas ! orkas !" * the people shouted—
Behold, a flock of huge gray birds,
Some mammoth sea fowls came approaching,

---

*An invented name for an imaginary sea fowl.

Swift running o'er the sands they came ;
With screeching noise their long wings flap-
      ping.
By a strong youth each bird was held,
With a cord beneath its wings tied firmly ;
They stood, a long and strange array,
For Arrah waiting to command them.—
Now heaved the sea tremendously,
And high upon the shore came rolling
The crested breakers foaming white !
Now seemed the sun to lose his brightness
As higher rose the sable clouds.
The youths competing took their places,
Each by a bird expectant stood ;
And each his hands had tied before him,
And 'round each bird was wound a cord,
Binding the wings close to its body.
On either side the course was marked
By cables, stretched to where the ocean
Had left his wave-marks on the sand.
The sky to southward quickly darkened,
The elements are up in arms,
And all the storm king's angry legions
Mid rolling thunder swept upon
Fair Eidolon !
      The orkas screech
As if in terror, louder, fiercer,
Their chorus mingling with the storm ;
As rolling, rising, angry billows

Now break upon the trembling shore.—
The signal for the start is given :
" Ho, Astaba !   Ho, orkas !   Go !"
Thus Arrah loudly cried commanding,
And onward speed th' unequal racers
Towards their goal upon the beach,
Towards destruction, towards death !
But ere they reached the goal expectant,
A monstrous wave came rolling leaward,
Engulfing youths and orkas all.
" Behold, behold !" cried Ideala,
" A god hath come from out the deep !"
With terror seized and fear, the people
With one accord her words repeat :
" Behold, behold, a god hath come,
A god is risen from the deep !
Oh, see him ride upon the billows,
Alas, alas, the youths are lost !"

CANTO V

I.

Man is but mortal, though his will
Be like a god's—strong and enduring ;
But harnessed to his flesh it shall
Be curbed into obedience.
                    Behold !
Upon his couch a weakened mortal ;
He who did brave the elements,
The ocean in its dreadful fury,
Here like a helpless child lies he,
Still battling in his wand'ring senses,
'Twixt hope and fear, and life and death,
A shipwreck on that awful sea.
Now hear him cry :
                    "Those eyes, those eyes—
Begone, thou gloating fiery demon—
O God, am I to perish here !
One drop of water, oh, some water—
A sail, a sail !—I see it—there !"
Then did he cast his eyes about him ;
Then half aloud unto himself:

"Where am I—ah, I was but dreaming ;
I'm safe, I'm safe—alas—

How strange !
Again, again I seem to see it,
That fair, that noble, queenly face—
Alas, 'twas but a dream, a fancy,
Those wondrous eyes' majestic fire
That left their mirage on my soul."
He ceased to speak, then looked about him ;
There Auma stood, his kind attendant,
Near him, with quick attentive eyes.
He looked at her in recognition,
And then a smile passed o'er his face,
Mute guerdon of his gratitude.
Then turning round, he saw before him—
His eyes could scarce believe it true—
One of his race, who thus addressed him :
"Good morrow, stranger, welcome here,
I'm glad to know you out of danger,
And glad to have companionship ;
I, like yourself, by adverse chances
Was cast upon this lonely isle :
My name is Lord Coquin, and with me,
Two others of my race were saved."
Scarce said, the stranger with emotion
Did grasp the hand of Lord Coquin :
"Oh welcome, welcome, noble stranger,
Scarce may I yet believe my eyes,
So like a romance seems this meeting

And all that happened me of late."
" Now rest you, I will call to-morrow,
When I would like to hear your tale."
Then to himself as he departed :
" Ha, ha, what speech was this he spoke,
While yet his feverish senses wandered
From this to that ?   Whom could he mean
But Ideala ?   Who else could have
That queenly face and look majestic ?
'Tis well, 'tis well, e'en as it is ;
'Tis well to note passing events."

II.

Arrah, beside his graceful daughter,
Was seated on his shady porch.
Calm was the morn, and still and warm ;
No breeze disturbed the leafy branches
Of the rich foliage growing near.
"This is the hour," Arrah addressing
His daughter, "when Lord Coquin should,
According to his promise, meet us ;
He hath, methinks, some message of
Good cheer from him, our youthful stranger."
To which his daughter answer made :
" Ah, fair is he, and proud his bearing,
And well he seems again and strong,
The stranger youth of whom thou speakest,
And whom I saw but yesterday ;
Full worthy of the highest honors,

If noble deeds go not unpaid."
" Sweet daughter, I have well considered,
And with the Mahib have agreed—
But see, Lord Coquin's servant enters."
" Ah, Monsieur Arrah, if you please,
My master's waiting for an audience,"
Spoke Maripo while bowing low.
" Go tell your master he may enter,
A friend is ever welcome here."
Before great Arrah and his daughter,
Lord Coquin bowed a grave salute.
" My noble Lord and benefactor,"
Quoth Lord Coquin, " I much rejoice
To see thyself and thy fair daughter
In prosperous health and peace of mind.
I've come to learn, if yet the Mahib
Is bent in purpose to accord
This stranger youth a public audience."
" He is, my brother," quoth Arrah,
" And all the chiefs so wish to have it.
A noble youth seems he, deserving
Some recognition from the state
For the great service he did render
On that unhappy festal day."
" May I but speak one word of counsel,
My brother and my friend—your pardon—
If from his speech I judge not wrongly,
This stranger is a plebian—
He has no claim by birth or station :

Nor may his worth be more than seeming ;
Let time first test his merit true;"
To which Arrah made answer boldly :
" I judge no man by birth or station ;
The deed he did, he did most nobly,
'Tis therefore I would do him honor."
"And here, beneath thy roof, dear father,"
Quoth Auma, "he hath shown to be
Full worthy of esteem and honor,
And all would like to hear from him
The story of his strange arrival ;
And how he saved with godlike strength
The helpless youths from certain death.
Didst thou observe how Ideala,
Whose eyes beheld the deed heroic,
Did speak in praise of the fair stranger,
And then and there made known her wish,
Just ere she left for Shalah's temple,
That he receive due recognition
Before the people and the state ?"
"'Tis even thus, my friend and brother,"
Arrah addressing Lord Coquin ;
" I own that thou art wise and noble,
Yet dost misjudge this stranger's heart."
Then stood Lord Coquin for a moment
In silence, ere he made reply :
" All this is known to me full well ;
Perchance I'm wrong, yet is my erring
No fault deserving of reproach ;

By large experience have I gathered
Some knowledge by the way,
Which makes me wary and suspicious,
And slow to place my faith upon
The things that may have but a semblance,
Concealing well deceit *within.*
Whatever have been my endeavors
My motive, pray, do not misjudge ;
My jealous friendship for thee only
· Urged me to speak without reserve ;
And I but hope he may be worthy
Thy friendship and thy high esteem."
To whom Arrah :

    "O friend and brother,
I thank thee for thy kindly council ;
Thou wilt be present, when to-morrow
The stranger in the hall of state
Shall speak before the great assembly ?"
"If it please thee I shall be there."
Thus saying Lord Coquin departed,
With inward chafing at the thought
Of failure in his undertaking.
In musings thus unto himself :
"A simple folk, and unsuspecting ;
They are as children, ever pleased
At novelties and outward show :
But there's a point about these women,
They share in common with the sex,
Their artful wiles and bland deception.

Well would fair Auma fain disguise
Her interest in the stranger's fortune ;
But blind were I, could I not see
The motive that controls her heart.
'Tis well for me, the Mahib's daughter
Sits in the temple of Shalah ;
Lest even she, more nobly gifted,
Of stronger mind, might fall a prey
To fickle passion's senseless ruling ;
And see in me (I own the truth,
For my gray hairs are past disguising)
A cold and time-worn man compared
With that adventurous, bold stripling,
Whose vigor and whose youth I own,
And handsome looks are in his favor.
But *art* and *strategy* are mine—
And mine shall be the price—I swear it !"

II.

The morrow dawned.   From far and near
Came people to the island city ;
For all had heard the stranger's fame
And of his marvelous arrival.
Within the spacious hall of state
The island chiefs were all assembled
O'er whom the Mahib did preside.
Near by the entrance, loudly talking,
Stood Blos O'Hare and Maripo,
Unmindful of the great occasion,

Unmindful of the surging throng
That grew from waiting much impatient.
"Ah, Mademoiselle Blos, *bon jour, ma cher!*
By Solomon, you do look charming,
And find you time to see this show?
My master says some tramp American
Would be the actor here to-day—
Hear you, a fraud, a common fellow,
So says my master."   "The plague o' yer
    master !
Ye are a pair o' rogues, sais Oi ;
An' ye, ye are a triflin' fellow
A-makin' light o' gintlemen
That's worth a thousand o' ye rascals.
Oi seen the lad, Oi hive, hear ye,
An' he's a noble boy, God bless him —
No more o' yer insultin' talk !"
Ere Maripo had time to answer,
Glad shouts were heard, " He comes, he
    comes !"
When from the throng arose a murmur
Of approbation and relief.
Arrah, the city's chief, now entered,
And at his side a noble youth,
Advancing straight unto the Mahib,
Arrah his speech began :

                    " Hark ye,
O chiefs and people here assembled !
No need have ye for empty words,

The cause ye know for this assembly.
Enough that I should briefly state
Th' event that on that day did happen,
When this our stranger guest arrived :
The word was given for the races,
And orkas and impatient youths
Together flew with heedless motion
Towards their goal precipitate—
When lo, from out the ocean rising,
An angry wave came mountain high,
And dashed upon the shore with fury,
Eng:lfing youths and orkas both !
Behold ! amidst the storm most dreadful,
(And who e'er saw such angry motion
Of all the elements before ?)
Amid the scenes and cries appalling,
There did we see this stranger youth
Give help and succor to the drowning !
From whence he came, or what his name,
Himself shall tell the story."

III.

       Then rose the youth
And spoke, the chief addressing :—
"Great Mahib, friends and citizens,
I am o'erwhelmed with gratitude,
Nor have I speech to give expressson
To the emotions of my heart.
Here do I stand, a lonely stranger,

Cast by the sea upon your shores ;
I have but done my simple duty,
Wherefor I claim no special praise :
But strange my tale is of adventure,
And how I came a shipwreck here,
This presently I'll mention.

                  'Twas noon :
Calm was the sea, e'en as you see it
Stretched out beneath this cloudless sky :
My ship lay on the placid waters,
As babe upon its mother's breast ;
The jolly crew 'mid song and pleasure
The lagging hours whiled away,
Nor had a thought or care of danger :
Secure our ship at anchor lay.
But like one roused from peaceful slumber,
With sudden rudeness, thus the cry,
'Ahoy ! Ahoy ! Ahoy !' rang startling
Upon the ears of all the crew.
Behold, a cloud of sable blackness
Portentous rose, and spread o'er all
The sky, by angry winds preceded !
A sudden change of scene ensued—
Each to his post the sailors hastened,
Obedient to their captain's call.
But 'gainst the elements rough warfare,
Man's works, his cunning and his art,
Are as poor toys crushed by some giant.
White-crested, high, against the walls

Of that black sky, the sea came rolling,
Resistlessly, with deaf'ning roar :
Sublimely grand in its mad fury,
Towards the trembling isle it came,
O'erwhelming ships of many nations
In one chaotic, awful gulf!
Meseemed my ship was crushed and shattered,
More know I not, for darkness fell
Upon me and did cloud my senses.
Ah, never may I know the fate
Of those proud ships that lay at anchor
Within the bay of *Samoa;*
Nor of my own, my gallant mates,
The noble laddies of the *Trenton,*
That served with me beneath the flag,
The proudest, freest flag a-floating,
A symbol of the brave and free,
On every sea beneath the skies,
The *Stars and Stripes,* my country's flag.

IV.

" But strange the truth, more strange than
    seeming,
That I should 'scape from that mad sea
And live, and here be 'mongst the living—
'Tis passing strange—'tis wondrous strange !
Much like a dream was my remembrance ;
Until my sluggish blood revived
And changed the compass of my reason.

When, clinging to an open boat—
Frail remnant of the noble *Trenton*—
I, sole survivor, found myself
Out on the vast and boundless ocean.
Above me shone the glorious stars,
Beneath, the sea seemed calmly sleeping ;
And I, twixt that immensity
Of sea and sky, was drifting, drifting—
I, a lonely mortal—drifting—
In that sublime and awful stillness
Drifting—I—alone—alone !
Enough ; speech fails me e'en attempting
To give expression to the thoughts
Of such o'erwhelming loneliness.
With the awakening day I noted
Great numbers of large sea fowls fly
Above me, bent in one direction—
A ray of hope shot through my soul ;
But hunger came and thirst upon me,
And mad'ning thoughts of wild despair ;
Ah, whither, whither am I drifting ?
Again, again, unanswered came !
Amidst the screeching noise above me,
A dark'ning cloud passed o'er my senses,
And then the blackness of oblivion—
Nor did I wake until I felt
Sharp, pinching pains upon my body.
I looked about me, when, behold !
Fierce eyes I saw upon me glaring,

With desperate effort then I clutched
And firmly held the feathered monster ;
I killed the bird and drank his blood,
And felt my waning strength reviving.
Thus did I live one change of moon ;
A gentle rain, too, having fallen :
My boat rode lightly o'er the sea,
For I had learned to use the power
Of those great birds to draw my boat—
Myself the bait, I caught th' ungainly
But useful birds an easy prey.
Nor was my reck'ning falsely founded ;
For, if from adverse winds preserved,
I hoped to be conducted safely
By my strange guides to some near isle.
Thus in my heart, each changing hour,
Fair Hope—dark Fear—alternate rose.
But lo ! from southward darkly rising,
Storm heralds dread approaching came.
All hope had vanished—my doom seemed
    certain.
Now rose and fell and tossed the sea,
My frail craft as a toy upholding ;
Resigned I did commend my soul
To the high Power above disposing.
Meseemed I lay engulfed beneath
The raging sea, when—how I know not,
Nor can I now believe it scarce—
I heard the cries of human beings ;

And then my feet touched solid earth !
Around me men were struggling, drowning ;
I cut the cords that bound their arms,
Then to my shattered boat all clinging,
We safely reached the welcome shore.—
Now here I stand, and crave your friendship,
I that am lost forevermore,
To loved ones, friends and kindred,
                              Alas,
A shipwreck cast upon your shore !
This is my plain and simple story—
Save, that I served my flag and country,
Holding an honored post of trust.
There's nothing more, kind friends, that I
Would care to add unto this story,
The simple story of Robert Lane.''

CANTO VI.

I.

'Twas in the noon of day ;
The rays no longer fell so fiercely
Upon two horsemen as they rode
Along their way in meditation :
Each had his thoughts, and silence seemed
Best comforter on this occasion.
Lord Coquin broke the spell at last :
" Ho, Maripo, seest yonder mountain,
Whose craggy peak is reared on high ? "
"I do, by Solomon, I see it—
But still, my stomach sees it not."
" I wish thine eyes were in thy stomach,
So thou couldst see its yawning depth ;
If thus thy appetite increases,
Thou soon wilt swallow all this isle."
" By Solomon, this is a stunner ;
My stomach thinks not so, my lord,
If Maripo must fast much longer
The isle will swallow Maripo ! "
"So be it then, as thou wilt have it ;

There is, so I myself perceive,
Substantial logic in thy folly.'
And here, here is a pleasant spot,
Here let us rest until to-morrow,
Near these dark woods' protecting shade ;
Drive up the ass with the provisions ;
Though yonder lies a village near,
Where we might meet with kind reception,
But as the night will be most fair,
We shall enjoy our out-door lodgings.
I will myself attend the steeds
Whilst thou a bill of fare preparest ;
And leave hast thou to do thyself
And thy capacious stomach justice."
No urging needed Maripo,
His native tastes were epicurean,
And proud he felt as *chef cuisin.*
With skillful hands he spread the luncheon;
Now all was ready, and he called
His master to the rustic board.
Awhile they ate in silence; when
Lord Coquin thus spoke to his servant :
" How now about thy stomach, sir,
Art satisfied and in good humor ?
There's something I would have thee know."
" *Bien*, my lord, and what's the humor ? "
" Canst count the moons since we are come
A shipwrecked crew upon this isle ? "
" I count the moons, my lord, say you ?

I count them daily upon my fingers—
I count them now—just eighteen moons—
Mon Dieu, mon Dieu! and how much longer,
My lord, it seems near eighteen years!"
"List, Maripo, to what I tell thee :
I'm weary of this dull go-round,
Yon city could no longer hold me ;
The living ever cling to hope,
Without it life's not worth the living—
Know'st thou, we may yet find a way
To 'scape from this our exile prison."
"By Solomon, if this were true,
Then Maripo would fast with pleasure,
And dance upon his head for joy !"
"Good !   Maripo, dost thou remember
Yon snow-capped mountain that we saw
Far off, in all its golden splendor ?
Towards yon mountain, and beyond,
As far as we may journey safely,
Shall we proceed, until I find
The farthest limit of this island,
Perchance another isle, or more."
Then Maripo with much excitement :
"Monsieur, my lord, you go alone—
By Solomon, no more adventures,
For Maripo hath quite enough.
No, no, my lord; I'm quite contented—
And then—there's poor Miss Blos O'Hare—
And monsieur young American—

No, no, my lord, I cannot go !''
" Hark, Maripo, a word of council
I know thou lovest Miss Blos O'Hare,
This is to me no longer secret—
And thou shalt have her—mark my speech,
For I am skilled in love affairs.
That she loves you, of that I'm certain,
And in thy absence will she more
Be bound to you by sweet affection.
'Tis woman's way to be perverse ;
For thy return will she be longing,
The while she thinks thee great and bold.
Then comest thou back crowned with new
    laurels,
And with a tale of daring deeds,
Of conquests and of strange adventures ;
A hero will she see in thee—
Thus play the game, and thou shalt win it.''
" By Solomon, I'll go, my lord,
I will be great, I love adventure—
But hark ! my lord, hear you not singing ?
By Solomon, I do, and there—
Mon Dieu ! a sober carnival !''
" Why man, move back and hold thy tongue;
They come this way, it is a funeral :
Thus do they carry here their dead
At night unto the funeral pyre—
Move back, move back, they come this way!'
" By Solomon, a funeral, sir !

An evil omen this, my lord."
Low chanting and with lighted torches,
The mourners slowly passed along,
Unmindful all of these two strangers.
Nor had Lord Coquin more to say,
But to himself thus fell to musing :
"This is the end, the end of all—
Why should my thoughts thus turn diverting
At sight of such a common scene,
Upon this subject dark and gloomy !
'An evil omen'—bah, poor fool :
A creature but of others' wishes,
A tool but fashioned for my use,
A thing that lives but unto others,
A creature but of circumstance !
To me there is no evil omen,
To me, who live and think and act,
And to my wishes and ambition
Make circumstances willing slaves !
The world is filled with dupes and fools,
That, dog-like, follow but their master,
And at his bidding fawn or bark.
Enough that I should know the motive
And purpose of my own affairs—
Let others be content at guessing
The while I execute my plans.
Now will they marvel and conjecture,
And wonder why I'm gone and whence—
But they shall be content at guessing.

One object have I, one alone,
And one full worthy my endeavors—
Ha, ha, 'tis well she sits secure
Behind the walls of Shalah's temple.
For twelve long moons will she be there,
In ministry unto her goddess,
The while on pain of death she shall
Behold the face of no man living !
Ha, ha, a virtuous vow indeed !
A vow, I own, quite in my favor;
Had I to frame this very creed,
Methinks I could not well improve it.
I love this proud and wayward lass
The more, because she seems to hate me ;
Not one of all the scores I conquered,
Seemed half as worthy of my pains—
But she's a woman, and like others
Must have the weakness of her sex :
And Lord Coquin shall yet subdue her.
And as to that vain stripling boy,
He's but a common, ill-bred fellow ;
Yet there's a brave and noble look
Upon his face, I own—but rashness,
If in my judgment I not err,
His rashness will be in my favor.
A hero dressed in common garb,
Soon will become a common object
Then will they see him as he is,
And by comparison I will profit.

An hundred chances, too, there are
He'll fall in love with Arrah's daughter—
But love's a game of chance—uncertain—
Who wins may lose, who looses may win.
That he aroused, when first I saw him,
When yet his brain was fever racked,
At mention of those 'eyes majestic,
That fair, that noble queenly face ;'
That he aroused a rankling hatred
Within my breast, I know, I feel.
Who else was it but Ideala,
Whom he beheld, though from the distance;
Yet 'twas enough to set his heart,
His fickle, fluttering heart afire.
And she, she too, so woman-like,
For ever by the new attracted,
Believed a god had come for certain ;
Her heart and soul were all excitement—
Did I not see it, even I—
Such things do not escape my vision.
'Tis this and that, when put together,
Will shape the outcome of this play.
Whate'er the end, one thing is certain,
I'll take no chances in this game.
On then, with boldness and with courage,
Ere twelve moons measure out their time,
Lord Coquin will return to conquer !
Ah ! there, already comes the queen !
How bright, how beautiful, and larger

Upon these southern isles she seems
Than in the northward latitudes!
Ho, Maripo! what's yonder fire?
Already sleeping—lazy wretch—
And dusky figures do I see
In circles slowly 'round it moving—
And hark! low singing do I hear—
Ye gods, it is is a funeral pyre,
A ghastly and ill-humored theme
For one to go to sleep upon.
But 'tis our common end—what difference,
If I do rot within the ground,
Be burned, or by the sea be swallowed,
Or whatsoever be the end—
Beyond there is no further knowing.
Enough that I should know to live
And make my life be worth the living."

II.

Dark is the night:
No star looks down upon the sea
That rolls and roars and raves and dashes
Its mighty waves against the cliffs,
As if to tear them down and bury
Their craggy heads beneath the foam.
But hark, amidst the storm, low moaning,
A human voice or hollow ghost
In plaintive tones complaining!
" *Mon Dieu, mon Dieu.* O Solomon!

Poor Maripo is slowly dying—
O wise one help poor Maripo!"
Then thus, another voice low speaking :
" Hold thou thy peace, I charge thee, fool,
If thou wouldst live, then be thou silent,
Lest thou awake this murderous crew
And fall a victim to their ire."
Spoke Lord Coquin, for well he knew
The nature of his savage captors,
Who, lying round about him, slept
The sound and heavy sleep of nature.
But reason hath poor Maripo,
This sleepless night for wailing ;
For there upon the ground they lay,
Poor Maripo beside his master
The captives of a barbarous gang.
The morning dawned upon them slowly ;
But even ere the sun appeared
Above the range of snow-capped mountains,
The natives rose and loosed the bands
With which the captives' hands were pin-
    ioned.
A hasty meal of fish and fowls,
Well roasted o'er an open fire,
Was soon prepared, but Lord Coquin
And Maripo had little relish :
For gloomy were their thoughts, and dark,
And hopeless seemed their fate impending.
Yet not a word escaped their lips,

Since taken by those rough barbarians ;
Lord Coquin neither quailed, nor showed
A sign of fear, when in their presence,
But every look and action told
A captive he, though yet their master,
Therein, he knew, his safety lay.
Again their weary march pursuing,
Lord Coquin and poor Maripo
Walked silently between their captors,
Along a high and rocky cliff;
Now climbing slowly, now descending
With cautious step some deep ravine.

                      At last,
When high the sun had risen,
They stepped upon a sandy beach,
And here beheld an inland bay
Expand its shining flood serene.
While far beyond, veiled in the shadows
Of wooded shores, an isle appeared
Like some fair form upon a mirror.
Though wan from hunger and fatigue,
Yet did Lord Coquin give expression
Unto his thoughts, as he beheld
This scene of loveliness and beauty :
"Most wonderful, most wonderful!"
" *Bien* my lord, I die of hunger,"
Quoth Maripo, " by Solomon,
Where does this crew intend to take us ? "
" Yet hold thy peace, and fear no more,

Methinks there is no further danger ;
But even much advantage may
Yet come from this, our strange adventure.''
''There, there, monsieur—but see, but see—
They come, they come, just see them rowing!
O Solomon, O Solomon !
I'll be murdered, I'll be murdered!''
A look of pity and contempt
Lord Coquin gave his frightened servant,
Just as the leader of the crew
Did order them their boats to enter ;
Then swiftly o'er the deep they sped,
And on the island's shore were landed.

III.

Albeit,

Where nature is most bountiful,
Man makes the least endeavor,
And living lives but to exist.
Thought Lord Coquin, when forth they led
   him
And Maripo unto the chief
Of these uncouth and barbarous people.
Within his wretched hut there sat
The monarch of his realm, surrounded
By dusky braves and sundry chieftains.
Without, a gorgeous flora wafted
Its sweet perfume o'er all the isle ;
Tall palms and festive clad asokas

Grew in luxurious splendor here.
Great fears came o'er poor Maripo,
When he beheld the grim assembly;
For he believed his end had come,
No mercy saw he in their faces.
Yet there was still his treasure left
To cheer and give him inspiration ;
He brought it forth, and opened it,
And 'gan to read his favorite author.
At sight of this, there came upon
The court a sudden agitation ;
Some forward pressed, and others fled,
And all seemed filled with dread alarm;
But Maripo still kept on reading
A chapter from King Solomon.
Now brought they forth another prisoner,
One who belonged to Mahib's isle,
Thus he to Lord Coquin made answer :
"The king commands that ye depart,
He fears you stranger's evil flower,*
And marvels much, not having seen
Upon his isle such as yourselves.
Were ye like me of Mahib's race,
Then would ye have to die to-morrow,
When prisoners from the Mahib's isle
Unto the gods are sacrificed.
Yet further counsel takes the king,
Until your fate shall be decided."

---

* Maripo's bible.

Now did Lord Coquin understand
The nature of his situation ;
Nor was he slow in making plans
To 'scape from his barbarian captors.
" List, Maripo, if thou wouldst live,
In all things do as I command thee."
" By Solomon, I'll do all that,
For I would live a little longer—
Poor Mlle. Blos—'twould break her heart—
Monsieur I'll do as you command me."
" I have no doubt of their intent ;
Thou seest how closely we are guarded ;
Force can avail us nothing here,
'Tis strategy alone can save us."

IV.

Alas !

But little sleep the prisoners had,
When with its golden splendor
Upon them dawned the fateful day.
The orb had risen high already,
When from the king the message came,
Demanding that the prisoners be
Led forth according to his summons.
While on their way, Lord Coquin saw
Great agitation 'mongst the people ;
With every step their numbers grew,
Until a vast concourse accompanied
The prisoners on their dismal way.

Upon an open field they halted,
And here again they faced the king
And all his court of dusky chieftains.
Before them in the glaring sun
They saw a field of strange white flowers;
But soon Lord Coquin's eyes discerned
The nature of this vegetation—
" They're human skulls," thus to himself,
" We're on the field of execution ;
These fiends would want to add more skulls
Unto this vast and shining pile."
Now drew the king his dusky soldiers
And stalwart warriors file by file
Around him in a semi-circle ;
Their numbers were surprising great—
To Maripo they seem ten thousand !
The prisoners bound, stood face to face
Before the king and his advisers ;
A solemn scene it was indeed,
For Lord Coquin and his poor servant ;
To add unto the ghastliness,
Some priests in flowing robes attended
The sacrificial flame around.
Upon command, two prisoners fearless
And soldiers two, advanced within
An open space ; the prisoners freed,
A cudgel unto each was given,
The natives' only weapon wielded—
Another sign, and now the duel.

Set teeth, and eyes aglow and fierce,
With cudgels raised, the conflict started
Amid the soldiers' deafening shouts.
Thus even did these fierce barbarians
Give their poor victims one last chance.
Lord Coquin and his trembling servant
Saw, one by one, the victims fall,
And dragged upon the smoking altar ;
Two left—now one—poor Maripo
Despairing, upon his knees had fallen ;
But Lord Coquin defiant stood,
The clumsy cudgel he refuses,
And like a panther, keenly eyeing
The slightest motion of its prey,
He stood, his trusty sword extended
Before his puzzled savage foe.
Now backward — backward — stepped the
     savage
With cringing motion, eyes aglow :
His weapon with swift motion rose
But harmless fell beside the victim.
Then pressing closer, step by step—
Quick as a flash, with motion studied,
Lord Coquin's sword straight to its mark
Passed through the body of his foeman.

CANTO VII.

ROBERT LANE PROSPERS IN ARRAH'S FRIEND-
SHIP — BECOMES ACQUAINTED WITH LIFE
ON THE ISLAND—GENTLE AUMA'S FRIEND-
SHIP.

I.

" Peace, O friend !
Leave now thy work, the day is done :
Another sun will rise to-morrow ;"
Broke on the ear of Robert Lane
The soft, sweet voice of Auma speaking.
" Meseems, I fear, thou hast of late
Been lonely here, O noble stranger ;
There's secret sorrow in thine eyes ;
This grieves me much, therefore have pity,
Confide thy heavy heart to me."
He ceased his work in Arrah's garden ;
For there before him stood the maid,
Who then his thoughts had been engaging,
Fair Auma, childlike, innocent,
Now leaning 'gainst a marble fountain,
Beside her placed a long-necked urn ;
Her large and lustrous eyes uplifted
Unto his own with quest'ning glance.
Her rhythmic voice and gentle manners,

And symmetry of form and face,
Stamped her a maid of grace and beauty
Enhanced by robes of spotless white.
Though young in years, but eighteen sum-
    mers,
Her knowledge and her learning was,
Her speech, her manners and her action,
In excess of her youthful age.
She had been kind and much devoted,
And taught with free unselfish zeal
All that she knew about her people
To Robert Lane, her hero friend.
Much had he need of such a teacher,
Poor shipwreck cast upon the isle,
Both as to customs, speech, and manners,
And the deep language of the soul.
The hero thus the maiden answered :
                " Welcome,
Auma, gentle friend !
Thou fairest of the island's daughters,
A guardian angel thou to me,
Dost ever cheer me by thy presence
And driv'st the darkening clouds away.
Believe me not, fair friend, ungrateful,
Because of this, my pensive mood ;
Thyself, thy father, and thy people,
Have been more kind than I deserve ;
To compensate in fullest measure
The gratitude I feel within,

Vain were indeed all my endeavors,
The span of life alas too short
Wherein to show myself full worthy
The friendhip of thy noble kin."
Then, silent for a time, they wandered,
The hero and his fair young friend,
Within her father's lovely garden.
Then did he take her by the hand,
And with a look of deep emotion
Gazed long into her large dark eyes,
The soulful eyes of Arrah's daughter,
And pleading thus his speech began :
" Believe me not, sweet child, ungrateful,
When in capricious moments I,
Oblivious of aught else about me,
Go wand'ring back into the past,
And there among old friends and kindred,
Among the scenes of happy days,
Do roam and dwell again in fancy—
Aye—for many a fond remembrance
Springs up, and draws me hence.
Alas, vain seem all aspirations,
When life's great purpose sinks beneath
The cruel sea of unattainment !
All this revolves within my mind
Much like a dream to me in seeming,
That oft I pause, forgot in thought.—
And yet, sweet Auma, 'mongst thy people,
I find a state, such as in fancy

I had created in my mind—
Yea, such as I had hoped and wished for
But deemed Utopian more than real."
" Albeit, how strangely thou dost speak ;
I scarce may ken thy meaning."

     " 'Tis well,
Sweet Auma, for to know brings pain ;
Thus ever, when one wish is granted,
Come other wishes, other hopes,
That fill the hungry soul with longing.
No single act of mine assisted
This noble state here in creating;
Hence do I feel the more abased
In sharing that I have not earned."
" Enough, my hero is forgetting
That I am his instructor here !
Away with all thy dreams and fancies;
Take life as thou dost find it, and
Enjoy the gifts of each sweet hour ;
Thus happy live, and free from care.
Thou hast in all things done thy duty,
What more wouldst thou or any one—
The morrow comes, live with the morrow,
Thus would I teach thee, noble friend,
The childish lesson of my life.
" Thou speak'st the truth, my kind instruc-
 tor,"
Thus Robert Lane, while to his eyes
A moisture came that gave a token

Of gratitude within his heart ;
With almost reverent tenderness,
He kissed her calm and queenly brow.
"Mayst thou, sweet Auma, find me worthy
To be thy grateful friend indeed."

II.

"Sweet daughter, thou hast well conducted
All the affairs placed in thy charge,"
Arrah his daughter thus addressing:
And while he spoke fell from his eyes
A fond paternal look upon her.
" Nor hath thy mother's watchful care
Found aught wherein to blame her daughter,
Though now it be nigh on three moons,
Since I did leave upon the mission
Required by the laws of state.
Well pleased am I, my wife and daughter,
To find all things thus well attended.
But tell me, child, how fares our guest ?
How thinkst thou now of him, my daughter,
Hath he performed his duties well ?"
Let mother speak of him, dear father,
Lest thou, forsooth, my speech misjudge."
" 'Tis well, 'tis well, leave now the answer.
I will myself see him ere long ;
And now, dear wife, and thou, my daughter,
I would be left unto my thoughts "
Thus Arrah to himself fell musing :

"As time doth judge all things aright,
Though slowly oft to our seeming,
Man's qualities are brought to light,
His worth, his virtues, or his vices,
Before time's judgment bar must render
A true account in his behalf.
Now will I seek this youthful stranger,
And if in merit he hath grown,
Then shall he duly be rewarded."

III.

"Me lad, God bless yer soul, good mornin'!"
Thus greeting spoke Miss Blos O'Hare
To Robert Lane whom she was seeking.
"I heard yer master had come back,
For 'tis the Mahib wants to see him ;
Oi hev a messige for yer lord."
" My good Miss Hare, I will conduct you
To Arrah, who has just returned—
But tell me, why have you been keeping
Yourself aloof these many weeks,
That I no chance have had to see you ? "
"Oh, bless yer soul, there's much to do
For me poor silf, since lassy's stayin'
In that old church o' yonder there—
An' ye hev niver seen me mistress ?
Och, she's a darlin' crature shure ;
Of course she cannot leave that temple—
A foolish haithen custom, sir ;

An' ivery day I be her messinger—
An' how she loikes to hear me talk
O' ye, the pretty darlin' crature :
An' then she sighs, an' looks so queer like,
An' says how she would loike to see ye."
" I'm pleased she still bears me remembrance,
For I too often think of her.
But listen, my good Blos O'Hare,
There are some things about this people,
That may to you and me seem strange,
Yet to themselves they have a meaning
As have our customs and our manners
To us in our native land ;
And more, Miss Hare, there is a purpose
In much that I have learned and seen,
A purpose is, about this people,
That does not stand for idle show,
Nor vain and senseless ceremonies ;
But springing native from the heart
Does ever seek man's higher state
In whatsoe'er they may be doing."
" Upon me soul, this is quite true,
Ye are indade a true American ;
The loikes o' me can't understand
Sich talk—but what Oi know, Oi know, sir,
An' there's no use o' argin this—
Me mistress is a darlin' crature
The loikes as niver lived afore ;
An if yer only could but see her,

Ye would jes' love her, she's so good !"
" My dear Miss Hare, no use in wishing,
Your mistress will yet some three moons
Remain in her secluded sanctum—
But here, here's this, this you may give
To your sweet mistress, Ideala,
In token of my high esteem."
"Yer picture, sir, an' shure its lovely !
Upon me soul, its loike yerself—
An' shure I'll give it to me mistress."

IV.

Now was great Arrah fully rested,
And now once more resumed his round
Of daily duties in his mansion
And through the city as its chief.
" A message here, and from the Mahib,
I must to him without delay."
Thus saying, Arrah left his chamber.
" But hold, I will not go alone ;
The Mahib thinks well of the stranger,
He shall with me to Mahib's court."
Then order gave unto a servant :
" Bring thou to me you stranger youth;
Bid him to come, Arrah commands it."

V.

The Mahib with his usual grace
Received Arrah and the young stranger.

" Tell me, Arrah," the Mahib spoke,
" How fare the people o'er the island ?
Are they well pleased with our rule ?
Are they enjoying full contentment ?
And how about our restless neighbors,
Have they invaded late our isle ? "
In answer thus Arrah replied :
                              "Great Mahib
I have learned while journeying
O'er all the island far and wide,
(And well and fully did I question
The chiefs and people everywhere)
Of no misdeeds nor ill-contentment,
Though there's some 'plaint against our
    neighbors ;
Save this, I found all prosperous peace.
The people do with cheerfulness
Perform their duties, heed our laws,
And praise the Mahib for his wisdom."
                              " 'Tis well,
Good Arrah, I rejoice
To hear from thee these gladsome tidings—
And now, how fares your stranger guest,
Will my young lord be pleased to answer ? "
" Great Mahib, pardon my poor speech ;
A debtor I to you e'ermore
And to good Arrah for your kindness."
" Great Mahib, my petition hear :
The frost of years is falling heavy

Upon my head, as thou dost see;
I feel life's winter is approaching,
And I must meet his stern command;
The gods decreed that I should die
Without a son as my successor
To share the burdens of my age.
Great Mahib, this our friend and stranger,
I deem a worthy youth, well tried
Most variously, and not found wanting;
Therefore, I deem it meet, that he
Should be commissioned my lieutenant,
A slight reward for noble deeds
Such as this stranger friend hath rendered."

VI.

"Oh!
This ever present Past,
That turns my thoughts back to my country;
That leaves a secret hopeless longing,
A constant yearning of the soul,
That no degree of honor can,
Or station, mitigate or temper!
Could I but hope, remotely hope,
To see again my own dear country,
And by one word or single act
Contribute to its many blessings,
Or from this, my experience, add
The smallest mite unto its progress:
Then might this yearning pass away

And I live happy and contented.—
But here—comes Auma—fair and sweet ;
I love her for her childlike manners,
And for her pure, unselfish heart—
And yet, there's seeming contradiction
'Twixt me and her—perhaps 'tis fancy—
But no—the compass of my heart
Points clearly to my course of action.—
Ah, here she comes, and singing too."
" Hail, stranger, hail, O friend and brother,
Lieutenant to great Arrah, hail !
These flowers here, so sweet and fragrant,
Accept from thy most humble friend."
"O Auma, kind and gentle maiden !
Though pure these sweet and fragrant flowers,
Thy heart is yet more pure than these—
And fairer than the fairest flower
Art thou, my sweet and gentle friend."

VII.

" And hast, my dear lieutenant, fully
Informed thyself upon this point ? "
" Most noble Arrah, thus they told me :
'Two strangers passed beyond the mountains,
Each on a steed was mounted, and
An ass did carry their provisions.
No other person followed them ;
Though nigh eight moons have run their
    courses,

" Away with all thy dreams and fancies,
Take life as thou dost find it, and
Enjoy the gifts of each sweet hour."

No tidings from them have been heard :
And from the rumors that are current,
'Tis feared, the Rhajabs* captured them.
All this, and other information,
Would indicate to me, my lord,
These were Lord Coquin and his servant.''
'' My dear lieutenant, much I fear,
There's truth in these ill-omened rumors,
Lord Coquin and his servant should
Have since returned unto the city ;
Lose now no time, but instant send
In search of them a well-manned party :
Instruct them as thou deemest best.
Well pleased am I with thy good service,
And much relief I find withal ;
Yet study patience and forbearance,
With wisdom coupled thou wilt learn
To do full justice to thy office.''
''My noble Arrah, light the work,
And full of pleasure are my duties,
Where all men aim and strive to do
Unto each other fullest justice.
Much have I wondered and conjectured,
That here upon this isle remote
A state I find of perfect pattern,
Such as I oft within my mind
In fancy to my seeming founded ;

---

* Name of semi-barbarians that captured Lord Coquin and
Maripo.

There's much that I would know and learn,
If thou wilt give me leave to question."
" 'Tis meet thou shouldst be well informed
Upon the history of my people."
" My native land, I own with pride,
Is one that gives unto its people
Full liberty and equal rights ;
There honest work and right endeavor
Find their reward in every sphere ;
There great men rise from humble stations
To highest honors of the state,
Where floats the flag of perfect freedom
O'er vast domains from sea to sea !
In all the arts of peace, my country
Among the nations leads them all :
It is the land, the home of freemen—
The legacy of blood and tears,
Cemented by the bonds of union
Into one common brotherhood."
To whom Arrah with thoughtful speech :
"If I not err, my dear lieutenant,
Then is thy country much like this,
Though still imperfect, yet expanding
In breadth and scope towards a plane
Where all men may live in contentment."
" My dear Arrah, in part 'tis true :
And yet, I note there is some difference,
Some difference—aye, 'twixt here and there,
As sunshine is to Hesper's beams.

In artful and inventive thought,
In enterprises vast, gigantic,
And in their boldness, push, and skill,
And in their daring execution,
They stand superiors in the world.
Misjudge not, kind Arrah, my meaning—
They lack the greatest boon on earth—
The boon of self-contentment.

                              Alas!

They strive and push and toil and scheme
For wealthiness with madd'ning fury,
As if the world nought else could yield,
And yielding which bring joy forever—
In their great eagerness they grasp
The husk, and throw the fruit away."

VII.

Arrah had listened with attention,
When thus he spoke with thoughtful speech :
              " My dear lieutenant,
There's much that thou hast said
That fills me with amazement,
And gives me cause for deep reflection.
What thou hast seen and learned since thou
Hast come upon this isle, lieutenant ;
The people and the state, and all,
All thou dost know of our laws,
Is writ and graven deep in hist'ry
Of blood and tears, and changeful times

Through many long and struggling ages.
Slowly the wheel of progress turns ;
Laborious is its every motion,
Until upon its upward course
A broader level is attained.
All thou hast told me of thy people
Meseems I fully comprehend ;
For here, here too, the same conditions
Among our people once prevailed;
A grasping, greedy, selfish course
Their sole endeavor and ambition,
That knew no limit save in death.
But I have learned to judge more kindly,
And view those things in reason's light.
Man has to rise from his estate
Of savage darkness, step by step,
And groping, plodding, find his bearings
Unto the light of brighter days.
Thus, as man's vision grows expanding,
Four epochs mark his upward course :
First, savagery through many ages ;
Then superstition's baleful reign ;
And then, alas, the heartless struggle
Of self for self against each other ;
And last, the Brotherhood of Man.
This state my people now have entered ;
For they have long since learned this truth:
Life is at best a fleeting journey,
And every wand'rer high or low

Must leave it poor, as he began it.
Thus whatsoever he would gain
Of worth intrinsic and enduring,
Not wealth nor power him can yield,
But acts that shall make others happy,
Works that by slow degrees shall build
The temple of true Brotherhood.
Besides the life that each is living,
There's yet another life within,
That soars to higher flights of vision :
That reaches far beyond the pale
Of human ken and vain ambition ;
That seeks alone supernal light ;
That hopes with Hope unwrit', unspoken ;
That clings to Love forever young ;
That knows life is no vain experience—
It is the life, the life Ideal,
The life that thrills betimes each being,
And stirs the soul with God-like thoughts !
As through the ages long and dreary,
Man, walking in his darksome paths,
Beholds at last the plain of knowledge ;
'Tis then he learns to know more fully
All that pertains to his estate.
Grieve not, therefore, my dear lieutenant,
The seasons have their time prescribed,
And man's affairs are ever changing
A cause for all—that none may change ;
The storm once o'er, a calm will follow,

And then a brighter day will dawn
For thy great country and thy people.'
Though ended had Arrah his speach,
When Robert Lane, yet meditating,
Sat silent, as if listening still ;
Then, with a look of deep reflection,
To Arrah thus these words addressed :
"Great Arrah, thou indeed hast spoken
The words of wisdom and of truth ;
My soul with hope renewed is kindled,
And life assumes a brighter hue."

CANTO VIII.

I.

Again
The Mahib's palace opened
Its doors unto a joyous throng ;
Fair Ideala left triumphant
The ancient temple of Shallah,
And re-united with her father,
Her young friends, gath'ring far and near,
With greetings came, and floral off'rings,
And many rare and precious gifts.
Upon a dais garlanded,
Surrounded by her lovely friends,
Sat Ideala, fairest daughter
Of all the daughters of Eidolon.
Sweet Auma, too, stood there beside her,
Her lustrous eyes now and again
Wand'ring about for some one absent ;
When, see! the blush tints on her cheeks
Grew deeper, and her eyes more bright,

As bending to fair Ideala,
She whispered, "There the hero comes!"
The city's chief and his lieutenant
Within the high arched entrance stood ;
Arrah himself his friend conducting
(Whilst every one stepped back a pace)
Unto the Mahib's gracious daughter,
And with a salaam grave and deep,
The hero to the maid presented.
This moment every eye was turned
Upon the two, as if a power
Unseen, celestial, were present.
How noble and how godlike he !
His deep blue eyes as if enchanted,
While his sealed lips no speech could find.
A moment thus stood he, then meeting
Her eyes, it seemed as if two stars
Had met, their ambient rays uniting.
He laid his gift of flowers, and then
From out the folds of his white toga,
He drew another, one that he
Above all else did prize and value :
It was his watch, by him received
While in the service of his country
In token of some noble deed.
This too he laid before the maiden,
Who with a gracious smile extended
Her hand, a mark of great esteem :
This, as the custom did demand it,

The hero kissed with reverence deep—
Thus did he meet fair Ideala.

II.

Like prisoner, freed from some dark dungeon,
Again beholds the light of day,
Delights again to freely wander
Through forest, meadow, hill and plain ;
Enjoys again to see the flowers
Greet meekly his enraptured sight;
Thus Ideala, blithe and happy
Walked through her garden late this eve.
Her heart was filled with strange emotions,
Such as she ne'er had felt before ;
'Twas happiness beyond her measure
With sadness tinged, she knew not why
Her heart should beat with such commotion,
Unless—howbeit, her crimson cheeks
Could not deny the story—unless—
And yet her heart would fain concede it—
For 'twas of him, she had been dreaming,
E'er since she saw him on that day
Come like a god upon the billows
Of that mad sea one year ago.
Again, how noble seemed his presence,
When late she met him face to face.
She paused, she listened for his footsteps;
Ah, will he come—ah, will he come—
How long the hours seem, how slowly

The Mother of the Night does rise."
Now standing 'neath a cassia's blossoms,
She looked toward the rising orb,
Absorbed in thought, when footsteps coming
Awoke her from her reverie.
"My Ideala!" thus the hero,
Then took the maiden's hands and looked
In silence into her dark eyes.
"I have been waiting for thee, brother,
How long the time seemed till thy coming,
Methought this hour had lost its motion;
Now do I thank thee for thy presence."
                    "Ideala!
Thine eyes so true, so pure,
Reveal the soul that dwells within thee.
O matchless queen! O maid enchanting!
If I within thy heart have found
One single thought, then am I happy."

III.

The power of love at last had conquered
The heart and soul of Robert Lane.
What long had been but idle dreaming,
What long had seemed mere fantasy,—
Now did he know and feel within him,
That he did love with all his soul;
That he did love a perfect being.
The ideal of his fondest dreams.
Long did they wander in the garden,

The lovers two, forgot in thought ;
For silence is the language when
The soul with soul holds sweet communion.
'' How lovely is this night how fair !
The very stars, the moon, seem brighter,
And all the isle a paradise.
Now do I thank my guiding star
That I was cast upon these shores :
Here would I dwell with thee forever,
My star, my love, my Ideala !
For when I saw thee on that day,
'Twas but a glance, yet 'twas sufficient :
Thy very eyes went to my soul,
There to remain a living image
Of my ideal forevermore.
But not one word, sweet, hast thou spoken,
That thou dost love me, Ideala ;
Why art thou silent, speak, oh speak ! ''
                          '' Be calm,
I charge thee, O my brother ;
Thou canst be happy—wouldst thou more ?
Thou shalt yet learn subdue thy passions—
Time is forever thine and mine ;
Then wilt thou learn, then only,
The value of true happiness.
Seest yonder orb, how pure, how lovely
She sails beyond the silent sea !
Much hast thou told me strange and beau-
     tiful,

Of other people, other lands,
That fills my childish heart with wonder :
Now would I have thou too shouldst learn
From me a simple story :

                      Yon orb
Is called the Mother of the Night ;
The sun, as thou dost know, is father
Of light, and all that is created.
There was a time, so wise men say,
When o'er this isle, though fair and lovely,
The savage beasts alone did roam.
The Mother of the Night, beholding,
Wept tears of pity and regret,
And thus the Lord of Day addressed :
"Thou hast made all things beautiful,
Yet wherefore, father, didst thou make them,
Wherefore this fair, this sylvan isle ?
These beasts and birds know not their maker,
And him that praise could give unto thee
Thou didst omit, the perfect being,
The noblest creature didst not make.'
The Lord of Day at last in pity,
Did grant the queenly mother's prayer.
'Behold,' spake he, 'I will create them !
Thy tears, into Lethena fallen,
Shall bring forth fruit, when thou again
Dost rise, fair Queen, behold thy children.'
Then rose the Lord of Day on high,
And with his golden wand did touch

The sacred waters of Lethena,
Into whose crystal flood had fallen
The mother's sad and piteous tears.
Therefrom arose two beauteous beings
Endowed with souls, that knew their maker,
Who thus became the ancestors
Of all the people of this isle.
'Tis said, so runs this ancient legend,
Lethena is a sacred lake
By Tasmin's * crystal waters fed,
Whose source lies in Nirvana : †
And Devachan‡ those may enjoy
That in Lethena's waters bathe.
But, born of tears, this heritage
Shall ever cling unto our race.—
Oft have I wondered since I know thee,
If this inheritance be shared
By thine own race and people ? ''
'' My sweetest Ideala :

                How strange
That thou shouldst ask this question ;

                  My people
Indeed are heirs to sorrow, yea,
Far more than thou couldst dream of Ideala.
But why this question, dearest ?
Enough that we this blissful hour
Be happy in each other's love.''

---

* A stream in Paradise.
† Heaven—a state of perfect peace.
‡ A felicitous state after death, when all that the soul craved
  for in life is granted.

Aye, even thus ; yet swift and transient
Like yonder clouds these hours fly ;
And knowing darker days will follow,
This knowledge then should make us stronger
To bear the future's fated burden.
Ah brother, I would have thee know
More of this story and its lesson.
As melts the dew drop on the grass
To find anon its place somewhere,—
You passing clouds, these trees, these flowers,
All teach this simple lesson, aye !
Canst thou discern, yea, thou dost surely,
For thou art wise, and thou hast faith—
Thus do they teach in Shalah's temple.
Though born of tears, the Lord of Day
Forever just and merciful,
Vouchsafed the state of blessed Nirvana
Unto the children of this isle.
And thou, thou too, my god-like brother,
Thou dost inherit his estate."
"May heaven grant me understanding,
Sweet Ideala, that I may
Divine the meaning of thy speech,
And that I ever may be worthy
Thy counsel and companionship.
Accept, sweet maid, my all, my being,
A suppliant before thy feet ——"
"Hush, say no more; good night my brother;
Time is forever thine and mine."

IV.

Upon the river's placid waters,
That 'round the city winds its course,
A lively scene of sport and pleasure
Amongst the people could be seen.
How fair, how balmy, and how dreamlike,
A summer's day upon this isle?
How redolent from myriad blossoms,
From fruit, and scented groves of palms,
Almost unto intoxication
The breath of zephyr fills the air!
An hundred pleasure boats disported
With pliant oar or flying sail,
O'er the smooth waters of the stream;
While laughter, song, and merry-making,
And gladsome voices everywhere
From shore to shore resound.

V.

But see!
Yon swan-shaped boat is slowly drifting
With idle oars adown the stream;
Nor song, nor laughter issuing
From the quiet occupants within.
A soft, sweet voice now breaks the silence,
Two dreamful eyes uplifted to
The pensive youth who sat beside her:
" My noble brother, why art thou

In melancholy thought abstracted,
When all the world about thee thrills
With laughter and with merry-making ?
In ill accord seem'st thou ; and yet,
Withal, I know there are such moments,
When deep within the soul alone,
Communion and self contemplation
Can find no words, no form of speech,
To give the throbbing heart expression.''
The speaker ceased; but list'ning still,
The youth sat there as if enchanted ;
Even as one, who, list'ning to
Some song, some melody entrancing
Still lists, when the last notes are fled,
With mute attention, till applause
Or sympathy can find expression.
Now did he lift his head, and bending
Toward the speaker, all his face,
His eyes, with deep emotion glowing,
His fair companion thus addressed :
'' Had I to ask of God one blessing,
One only favor, and no more ;
And this one blessing being granted,
The one for all eternity ;
It would be this, the only blessing
That I would crave, and this alone :
That I might thus forever listen
Unto the sweetest, dearest voice,
And thus forever look with wonder

Into thy deep enchanting eyes :
Why not these too, as stars are shining
With radiant glory in the skies ! ''

VI.

'' Judge not thus rashly, O my brother ;
Though every day may bring its joy—
Not every joy succeeds another ;
The pleasures of the yesterday
May mourn some grief to-morrow.
                              None knows—
But hoping ever wings the soul
Its circling flight from flower to flower,
Like the fantastic butterfly
Sipping the sweets from every chalice. ''
'' O Ideala, fair and good,
Thou speak'st as sage hath never spoken ;
Grant I may add one single thought
That now my heart would crave expression :
How lonely would this fair world be,
With all its sweet and lovely flowers,
Were there one only butterfly
To wing about the nectar sipping ?
Grant, Ideala, that I too
May join thee in thy flights supernal ;
May join my heart my soul with thine.
Knowst thou, O fairest Ideala,
If ever human soul hath loved
With all the passion, hope, and fire

That human soul may hope to love,
Thus I, I love thee, Ideala!"
" Ah brother, I scarce comprehend
The meaning of thy speech, though truly
I deem thee noble and sincere—
But hark ! but listen !—some commotion
Within the city do I hear—
Grant that the dreaded dark-eyed stranger
May not already be returned."

VII.

Auma, sweet child of lighter mood,
Taking all life's affairs and changes,
Light-hearted as the warbling lark,
Prepare !   Alas, a storm is breaking !
Lest it shall break thy heart, poor child,
Aye, break thy heart—for love is cruel,
And first sweet love to lose forbear—
What bitter, bitter sorrow !
                                        Auma,
Locked close within her own apartments,
Thus gave expression to her grief :
Alas ! now I do know this feeling
That thrills betimes my very soul ;
That sends the hot blood coursing, rushing
Through all my veins tumultuously;
That makes my heart beat fast and faster,
And fills my thoughts with strange delight !
'Tis ever thus when I am near him,

And thus when e'er I hear his speech—
'Tis he, 'tis he, my hero-stranger,
'Tis he I love—'Tis he alone !
But oh, my heart. why thus rebellious,
Wherefore dost give me all this pain ?
Thou hast ne'er thus with grief oppressed me
At thought of him, as thou dost now—
But then, O gods ! have I not seen him
With Ideala yesterday !
And thou, my heart, dost tell me truly
He loves her and he loves not me.
His speech, 'tis true, ne'er gave me token,
Therefore my heart must be content
To love him, though he love another.''

VIII.

With cymbals and with sounding drum,
Lord Coquin and his servant entered
The city with some fifty youths,
That Robert Lane, Arrah's lieutenant,
Had sent towards the snowy range
In search of the long-missing strangers.
'Twas this that Ideala heard ;
That filled her soul with dim forebodings;
Whereat she ceased her speech and fell
Into a mood of meditation,
A dreamlike, listless reverie.
In vain did Robert Lane endeavor
With cheering words to rouse his love ;

She only begged that he conduct her
Straight to her home, the Mahib's court.

IX.

Lord Coquin's long, mysterious absence
Was still the topic of the day :
For soon the wand'ring news had traveled
The rounds of every house and cot :
And people wondered and demanded
That he before the Mahib tell
The story of his strange adventures.
Nor was the happy Maripo
Less anxious than his lord and master
For this great day, that unto each
Should bring the hoped for recognition.

X.

A happy day indeed it was
For Maripo, who had found favor
Within the eyes of Blos O'Hare.
For she did listen to his story
With marked attention, yea with pride ;
Of deeds heroic and adventures ;
Of his great coolness, prowess, and
Great valor, and escape from dangers,
Yea tortures, and horrible deaths !
" I' faith, ye are indade a hero,
Sich as Oi'm plased to hear and see,
An' bless me soul, i' faith, Oi wonder
There's left a bit o' ye at all !' "

XI.

" Mademoiselle Auma, please, me lady,
Me master, Lord Coquin, did send me :
He would be pleased to see me lady
Upon some business of import."
"Go tell thy master I send greetings,
And ready wait his coming hither,"
Auma the ready answer gave
To Maripo, Lord Coquin's servant.
" This little man seems very strange,
But yet more strange to me his master—
There's something in his very nature
Beyond my simple understanding ;
Though father thinks well of this man,
To me he's vile, repugnant.

           What mission,
Forsooth, directs him hither ?
I scarce can guess his aim or purpose !
But here he comes—how proud he looks !"
" Ah, fair and gentle friend, sweet Auma,
Accept my thanks for kindly welcome !
To thee my first steps are directed,
To learn what may have passed, perchance,
Since I went forth upon my journey.
How fares it with the stranger lord,
The young lieutenant, Robert Lane ?
Methinks, if right I am at guessing,
Hath he not won sweet Auma's heart ?
Fear not, sweet maid, so bold a question,

But answer make thy honest friend."
"Lord Coquin, pray, is this the burden,
The object of this mission?

                "Aye—
There may be more, my gentle maiden."
"Then will I frankly tell thee, sir,
The young lieutenant loves my friend,
And is of her beloved again."
"But is this only to thy seeming,
Or hast thou proof of what thou sayest?"
"Had I no proof, I should not say it:
But yesterday my ears received
Convincing proof of this my statement."
"But here — but here — what's this, sweet
     Auma—
How come you by this photograph?"
"A simple chance—'twas Ideala's:
She showed it me, and here forgot it:
'Twas give to her by Blos O'Hare,
While yet a queen in Shalah's temple."

XII.

Lord Coquin sat within his chamber,
Absorbed in moody thoughts, alone,
When from the Mahib came the summons
By special messenger conveyed,
That he, Lord Coquin, was expected
To tell the people and the chiefs
The story of his strange adventures,

Whilst journeying 'mongst the savage tribes.
With firm and haughty step he entered,
Conducted by the city's chief,
And Robert Lane, his young lieutenant.
Around the Mahib sat the chiefs :
And the great hall was thronged and crowded
With an expectant multitude.
Lord Coquin, bowing to the Mahib,
His speech began with firm, deep voice.
His journey first told, then his capture,
And how, upon the sanguine field,
The victims, by the savage chieftain,
Were sacrificed unto the gods.
" My turn, and that of my poor servant,
Soon came," Lord Coquin spoke ; then drew
His trusty sword to show more fully
How he did wield it in the strife.
" Unused to such poor seeming weapons,
My adversaries, one by one,
Fell dead upon the field of contest.
Nerved for the fray, I held my ground,
And not until three score had fallen,
Did they indulge a moment's truce.
Then, quickly turning to my servant,
By secret art, known but to me,
I set in flames his withered flower;*
Which, snatching, I thrust in my mouth,
And from the smoke and flames and fire,

*Maripo's bible.

I then drew forth a silken cord ;
Which, winding 'round my servant, I
By word mysterious did command :
When lo ! a serpent did uncoil,
Of monstrous length and shining colors,
Which, straight towards the Rhajabs' chief,
With hissing sound its fork extended ;
Whereat, the soldiers, chiefs, and priests.
In headlong flight the field deserted,
Leaving us the victors of the day.

XIII.

" Now could we wander at our pleasure,
In safety o'er the Rhajabs' isle ;
The which we did, and for a purpose.
Already had I seen and learned,
That these uncouth and savage Rhajabs
Were enemies to this fair isle :
And now, e'en now, there is some danger,
O noble Mahab and ye chiefs,
There's danger that this savage people,
Unguarded, may invade your realm ! "
Lord Coquin now his speech concluded,
Did, from the Mahib and the chiefs,
Receive spontaneous gratulations,
And demonstrations of esteem,
From all the people 'round about him.

CANTO IX.

I.

"Peace !
I've summoned thee, Lieutenant,"
Thus Arrah spoke to Robert Lane,
"To counsel with thee o'er some matter
Of grave import unto the state.
Whilst I have neither cause nor reason,
To doubt Lord Coquin's story, or
Impugn his motive or his purpose ;
Yet am I not in full accord
Within myself concerning him,
Or his adventures, or his stories,
Or threatened danger from our neighbors.
Yet do I deem it best, that we
With Lord Coquin confer in person,
In order that he may explain
More fully the true situation."
          Thus Robert Lane :
"Good Arrah, thou

Need but command me in this matter;
For thou know'st best all that concerns
The state, whilst I could be but guessing,
What wisdom and experience have
In thee adjusted and perfected."

II.

"Monsieur, my Lord Coquin, beg pardon ;
The chief and the American
Have come to see Monsieur my master."
"Go, Maripo, bring thou my sword,
Then tell them they may enter.
                              'Tis well,"
Thus to himself, " I guessed aright,
'Tis well—'tis well—my plans are working—
I have not risked my life in vain,
Nor vainly urged into sedition
And deadly hatred and revenge,
That savage crew beyond the mountains—
As slips a mouse into a trap,
Shall my fine fellow thus be baited.
Ah, noble Arrah, welcome here,
And welcome too, Arrah's lieutenant."

III.

" Peace and good health to thee, my brother!
We've come upon some errand that
Concerns the state and all my people ;
Tell me, good brother, all thou knowest

About the Rhajabs' base intentions."
" 'Tis well, 'tis well, my good Arrah ;
Accept first my sincere expressions
Of lasting gratitude, for thy
Most gracious favors and attention,
For timely succor and relief.
What I have learned from observation,
While on the Rhajabs' distant isle,
Leads me to draw the firm conclusion
That they some mischief have in view ;
And what is more, they're well recruited,
And cunning, e'en as they are fierce.
Methinks their object is for plunder,
And prisoners for the sacrifice."
" My brother, what wouldst thou advise,
What plans, what steps to take, what
    measures,
To thwart the Rhahjabs' bold designs ? "
" My noble Arrah, if suggestion
Can be of service, then would I
Advise the borders to be guarded ;
And forthwith drill and organize
A force sufficient to be ready
Upon alarm to crush the foe.
I will myself, with thy lieutenant,
Provided he's no craven heart,
Take part in this, thy expedition."
Quick as a flash, the hot blood rose
Into the face of Robert Lane :

But Arrah rising, he repressed
The burning fire within his bosom.
"My friend and brother, thanks I give
To thee for thy advice and counsel ;
Come, my lieutenant, let us make
Arrangements for the expedition."

IV.

With energy and skill and tact,
Arrah's lieutenant had completed
All details and arrangements for
The expedition to the mountains,
Which he himself was to command.
"Now will I," thus unto himself,
"To Lord Coquin; he shall not suffer
To go unpunished for his taunt,
His insolence in Arrah's presence.
That he should hate me, I can scarce
Perceive a valid cause or reason,
Unless 'tis envy—or perchance—
But no, I will not groundless foster
A jealous thought within my breast."

V.

"Monsieur, my Lord, 'tis the lieutenant."
"Ah, 'tis well, 'tis well you've come ;
My dear lieutenant, how's your master?
And his fair daughter, eh, how's she?
And how your military tactics ? "

"Lord Coquin, you need not be worried
Concerning these or my affairs ;
My business here is to inform you
That all is ready for the start,
And you, by Arrah, are commanded
To lead the forces in reserve.
If you're a gentleman or soldier,
Now ere we start, I challenge you
To stand upon the field of honor,
Or own that you're the craven heart ;
This is my business with you now."
"Ha ha, ha ha, my dear lieutenant,
Let not your angry passions rise—
Be not too hasty ; spare your feelings—
The state could ill afford to lose
Your services, my good lieutenant—
First to the war, and when 'tis over,
And neither slain by other foes,
Then am I, mark you, at your service.
But first, pray, what degree or station,
What noble family claims your name ?
For I would deem it most abasing
To measure swords with common fellows !"
Now to his feet sprang Robert Lane,
His eyes with indignation burning ;
Quick as a flash he drew his sword—
"Take this," he cried, but Lord Coquin's
Quick eye the blow anticipating,
With counter motion parried well

The threat'ning steel of the lieutenant.
" Enough," spoke Lord Coquin, " enough;
I own you are a gentleman."
" And more," thus Robert Lane retorted,
" I served beneath the Stars and Stripes;
I am—and proudly do I own it—
One of its sovereign citizens;
No other title do I boast
Save that I bear an honest name !"

VI.

The soft still night had wrapped her mantle
Of pearly stars o'er sea and isle.
No sound was heard, save the deep breathing
Of ocean's heavy lab'ring breast;
When suddenly, the stillness breaking.
The great drum in a martial strain,
With e'er increasing sound of thunder,
Did startle Nature from her sleep.
"To arms ! to arms !" the herald shouted,
And soon the quiet city woke
Into a life of animation.
The Mahib, Arrah, and the chiefs,
And Robert Lane the young lieutenant,
The heralds' messages received :
" 'The Rhajabs have been seen advancing
In great force through the mountain pass."
Thus Arrah read one herald's message.
' Do not delay, but send at once

The needed troops to our assistance.'
' Send all reserves without delay;
The Rhajabs swarm the mountain passes.'
These are the tidings,'' Arrah spoke ;
Then to his young lieutenant turning :
'' How soon canst thou proceed to march
With haste, and yet in perfect order ? ''
'' Ere yet the Lord of Day doth greet
The brazen tower of Shalah's temple,
Shall all the troops in order leave
Toward the destined field of battle ;
I do commend myself to thee,
And to the Mahib and the elders.''
To whom the several voices thus :
The sun, personified—here, invoked, to lend
    his good influence.
'' May Ra* protect the brave lieutenant !''
'' May fortune smile upon thy brow !''
'' Mayst thou return with vict'ry crowned !''

VII.

One only star with radiant lustre,
Bright Venus, lovely Queen of Morn,
Hung trembling o'er the gray horizon,
As if she feared the throbbing sea
That darkly lay beneath her path.
One pair of eyes, all sad and thoughtful,
Gazed through the silence of the night,

---

* The sun personified—here invoked to lend his good influence.

At you bright star in dreamful musings,
As if in sweet companionship.
How like a fairy, how enchanting,
She looked in her white flowing robes,
Beneath the vines of sweet dendrobium
That clust'ring hung from stately palms!
The whidahs, startled, left their perches :
A pet gazelle looked shyly 'round
At the unusual vision.
     " This is the hour !
Bright star, soon will thy journey
Take thee beyond yon dark deep sea—
But though obscured and sunk from view,
Thou dost arise with new-born splendor !
Oh could my heart thus hope to rise
From this dark hour of love's first sorrow!
Ah, will he come —alas,
Impatient grows my heart and lonely."
      Scarce said,
The hero's form appeared,
And to his bosom pressed the maiden :
" My own, my only Ideala !
Hast thou, oh dearest, long been waiting ?
A god should this thy pain requite !
O blissful hour alloyed with sorrow ;
My love, my own, my Ideala !
Scarce have I anchored in Love's haven,
When I again must leave his port,
To sail upon life's changeful sea

The hour is come—my Ideala ;
I must depart as I'm commanded—
Yet shall our hearts not be divided—
Farewell—farewell, sweet Ideala !"
" Yea fare thee well !   Though there may
    come
Deep sorrow to thy heart and mine—
I know it, oh my brother-lover,
There's sorrow will come o'er us both—
But as you star will rise to-morrow,
Our plighted faith shall shine anon
More brightly in love's promised skies."

VIII.

'Twas passed one moon since Robert Lane
Had started for the field of conflict ;
When Ideala, hearing naught
Of tidings from her absent lover,
To Auma hied, her bosom friend.
" Peace be with thee, O Auma, sister !"
Then looking deep into her eyes :
" Alas, thou too dost grieve, my sister:
Thine eyes some sorrow do betray—
Hast thou too from some lover parted ?
Oh tell me, Auma, hast thou yet
No tidings from the seat of war ?"
" None yet, my dearest Ideala."
Then smiling faintly in disguise:
"Oh dearest, mine is but the sorrow

Of sympathy for other hearts—
A passing cloud, sweet Idéala.
No, no, I have no absent lover,
For I'm not loved, dear Ideala."
"And yet thou too dost love him, Auma,
I know 'tis true, 'tis writ within;
Thou lovest him, Auma, e'en as I :
And who's the maid that could not love him,
For he's a noble man indeed !
Oh, calm thy heart and love him, Auma,
For pure sweet love loves not in vain,
The Alsi sijil* will record it,
And thine, thine shall be devachan. †
But why dost bend thy head in silence?
Hast thou no answer for thy friend ? "
" No answer have I, Ideala."
" Then list, my child; for I did dream
An evil dream that bodes me ill,
And ill, I fear, unto my lover :
Within a quiet forest glade,
An antelope and mate were browsing
Upon the sweetest morsels that
A plenteous forest offered freely :
It was a sweet and pleasing sight.
Alas ! as if by sudden magic,
E'en as I looked, my eyes beheld
A crouching panther spring upon them,

---

* Recording angel.
† A felicitous state ofter death when all that the soul craved for
   in life, is granted.

His murderous teeth deep in their flesh
And in their vitals tearing—
                              When lo !
An ambushed huntsman, but too late,
An arrow sent upon its errand,
That pierced the murderous panther's heart.
But hark! but hark! what mean these blasts?"
" The soldiers from the field returning ? "

IX.

Once more the great drums wildly rang,
And everywhere the people gathered
To hear the heralds cry the news :
" They come ! they come ! the war is over ;
The victors come, the day is ours ;
Long live Coquin, the conquering hero ! "
Nor had the people long to wait,
To greet the soldiers now returning :
But Lord Coquin, on his black steed,
Not Robert Lane, the young lieutenant,
Rode at the head of all the troops.

X.

Lord Coquin's deeds of valor spread
Throughout the city and the island,
And every tongue his praises sang,
Save three; these in their hearts condemned
The hero as a traitor base.
These were the sorrowing Ideala,

The gentle Auma, and Blos O'Hare.
Once more within the Mahib's palace,
A festive throng was gathered 'round.
To hear Lord Coquin tell the story
Of conquest and heroic deeds.

XI.

Lord Coquin, with his usual pomp,
Before the Mahib told this story :
"The troops, by the lieutenant placed.
In line of battle, were awaiting
The Rhajabs from the mountain pass :
A forest deep our rear protected,
And 'long the causeway. where the foe
Would pass, 'twas deemed to gain an
    entrance :
There with my force I lay in wait
To intercept the advancing foe.
But great was our surprise, at seeing
The enemy turn and defile
To northward in a move strategic.
The young lieutenant, seeing thus
His plans frustrated and outwitted.
Gave the command for an attack.
Leading himself the soldiers onward.
It was a brave and gallant charge :
But. unaccustomed to such warfare.
The bold lieutenant and his men
Were driven back into the forest,

And sorely pressed, when with my forces
I hastened unto their relief.
Methinks it was in this fierce struggle,
The brave lieutenant wounded fell.
Soon was the tide of battle turning ;
The Rhajabs routed, took to flight,
And in dismay and in confusion,
Made for their mountain's safe retreat.
Though long pursuing them, we captured
But few of the retreating foe;
Their hiding in the wild surroundings
Made difficult pursuit and chase.
Returning to the field of battle,
Our long and patient search did fail,
To find among the dead or wounded
The body of my servant, or
That of the valiant young lieutenant.
I grieve their loss, and all the more,
Because these savage Rhajabs offer
Their fallen foes unto the flames.''
His speech concluded, thus the Mahib
These words to Lord Coquin addressed :
'' The state decrees to thee, my Lord,
For the great service thou hast rendered,
The high degree of Astaba,
Whereby thou art henceforth admitted
To all the counsels of the state.''
'' Long live Lord Coquin !'' voices shouted
From everywhere throughout the hall.

CANTO X.

I.

Who e'er has loved
With Love's first passion deep, enduring,
And buried Love's sweet hope for aye !
Who e'er has loved, and stood beside
The still, white form of his dead love,
May know the silent grief of griefs,
The voiceless, tearless pang,
The hopeless void, the deep despair
That naught on earth can mitigate !
                    Ideala,
Though conscious by prevision
A fateful issue of her love ;
Though knowing love by sorrow tempered,
Exalted grows and fairer still—
Alas, poor heart ! unused to sorrow,
How keen thy pain, how deep thy grief !—
The dawn just broke, when Love's fair morn
With threatening clouds grew dark.
                    " He dead !
No, no," thus to herself consoling;

"It cannot be, he is not dead—
It cannot be—he must be living—
My heart tells me he is not dead !
There is some plan meseems, some plotting,
By envy fostered, that would keep
My hero from me and the city.—
My dearest, hast good cheer for me ? "
Her maid, Miss Blos O'Hare addressing.
" Och darlin', no, Oi've only come,
Because yer father wants to see ye."
" I thank thee, Shining Face ; hast yet
No tidings from thy own lost lover ? "
" No, darlin', no ; it breaks me heart
To think they're makin' roast beef of him."

II.

" My daughter, I am pained to see
Thee thus consumed with silent sorrow ;
Much have I hoped that time would heal
The wound inflicted by war's chances.
My daughter, thou must learn to live
Compliant with life's various ways ;
Leave the bygone unto the past,
And live to-day, and for the morrow."
" My father, thou dost wrongly judge ;
I loved but once, and loved most truly,
With all the passion of my heart :
With all my soul, with all my being,
The idol of my first love's dream.

And he, he too, my love returning,
Loves me with that sweet holy love
That neither time nor earth nor heaven,
May blight or sever or expunge ! "
" List Ideala, I, thy father,
Would know thee happy, for thou knowest
Thy joys are mine, and mine thy sorrows.
Now have the weighty years bowed down
My head as with a heavy burden,
And I must tell thee, frankly too,
Of something that concerns me deeply :—
Thou knowst the Lord Coquin is now
A hero honored, and his station
Ranks him an equal with our chiefs :
And he doth love thee, thus he tells me,
And for his consort asked thy hand."
"And I, dear father, I do hate him—
His heart is cold, and black his soul—
And Ideala, I, thy daughter,
Can never be his bride ! "

III.

                    " How now !
'Tis well, my pretty bird, 'tis well,
I soon will have thee in my power ;
'Tis well I learned this barbarous speech ;
'Tis well I learned from these old volumes
The silly laws and customs hard,
That I, by evidence convincing,

May bring this haughty maid to terms.
A photograph, ha ha, I have it !
How little dreamed that youthful ape
That this, his photograph, would help me
To crush his own sweet lady love.—
Ah, here they come—now to this business.
My friends and brothers, peace with you ;
This is indeed a grievous hour
That calls your council here to-day.
I'm pained to lay before your honors
The evidence of broken vows,
And all the more, because it threatens
The daughter of our highest chief ;
But who will want to own obedience
To church or state, when 'tis found out
That, in the highest ranks, vile treason
Is practiced and our laws defiled ! "
" Lord Coquin these are heavy words
Deserving of investigation ;
Let's know the cause of thy complaint."

IV.

" My friends and brothers, list and learn :
When the fair daughter of the Mahib
In Shalah's temple reigned a Queen,
'Twas then her sacred vow was broken."
When several elders thus, amazed :
"A grave and awful charge, O brother,"
" Here is the evidence ; my lords,

Know ye this likeness ?   'Tis the shadow
Of Robert Lane the young lieutenant ;
Though but a shadow, yet the face
Of him is real as life itself.
This did she have while in the temple,
And oft beheld it with her eyes;
Her maid, the Shining Face, did take it
Unto her mistress in the temple ;
And I, from Auma, her dear friend,
Obtained it but few suns ago."

V.

In a forest dark and gloomy,
There stands the huntsman's lowly hut;
No voice is heard save the low sighing
Of evening breezes in the trees ;
The light of day, though slowly fading,
Yet had the huntsman not returned.
But list ! within the hut, low voices
The awful stillness almost startle !
Upon his couch of ferns and rushes,
Lay Robert Lane, Arrah's lieutenant,
Emaciated, pale, and wan,
His noble features seeming older
Beneath the mask of his dark beard ;
While, bending o'er him, Maripo
With anxious care his patient tended.
" Thanks, Maripo, this cooling draught
Allays my racking, burning fever,

And brings the wand'ring senses back
Within the compass of my reason.
I'm stronger, Maripo, I'm stronger—
And now, my dear good Maripo,
Do tell me all, the whole sad story,
Of how I came unto this place—
Oh how I dreamed, and dreamed ! but
    dreaming,
Yes, only dreaming, saw my love,
My goddess, my lost Ideala ! ''

VI.

Monsieur lieutenant, I will tell ;
But first, Monsieur lieutenant, promise
Not to betray me, nor to use
Me as a witness 'gainst his lordship,
My former master, Lord Coquin ;
For he is bad and bold and scheming,
And he would kill me, he would kill—
O Solomon ! and that, Monsieur,
Would break my darling's heart.
                              Now listen :
For I, I Maripo saw all,
O Solomon! I'm bold and daring,
And when Monsieur lieutenant made
That charge against the savage Rhajabs,
I hid behind a friendly tree
To watch the cunning foe the better—
'Twas then, *mon dieu,* 'twas then,

That Lord Coquin, my former master,
Rode up; when all the savage crew
Did turn upon Monsieur lieutenant
As if by pre-appointment—ah—
But in your ear this must I whisper—
He did not lift one hand to save
Monsieur lieutenant from his foes
Then, as the field of battle changed,
I, quickly on my shoulders bearing,
Did carry Monsieur to a place
Of safety here in this deep forest ;
'Twas then I met the huntsman, who
By chance appeared, and who did take
Monsieur lieutenant to his hut."
" Ah, Maripo, an honest fellow !
Give me thy hand, an honest hand,
And let me press it with deep feelings
Of gratitude and fellowship.
Fear not the vengeance of thy master,
He shall not have a chance to hurt
One single hair upon thy head."

VII.

The very heavens seem to darken
With cloudy vengeance on this day,
That brought upon the Island City
The deepest sorrow of the age.
The people stood in groups assembled,
And talked in solemn tones and low,

And looked despairing at each other,
And shook their heads, and said no more.
All seemed to feel the fate impending;
All seemed to know the awful doom
That the harsh sentence of the judges
Would bring upon their idol Queen.

VIII.

The judges in the hall of justice,
Old Ageram, the chiefs and scribes,
All looked with eyes stern and command-
    ing
Upon Lord Coquin, who did bring
The awful charge against the daughter
Of their beloved chief.
                        He showed
In evidence the hero's picture,
And held it up that each might view
The image to his satisfaction ;
Then with loud voice he thus proclaimed :
" This is the likeness, noble judges,
The face that your beloved Queen
Did look upon while in the temple—
And here, these are my witnesses,
Fair Auma and the Shining Face,
Let these, I pray, tell their own story."
" What hast thou, Shining Face, to say ? "
Thus Ageram now spoke commanding.
" Yer honor, what Oi hev to say

Is only this—that man's a villain,
A lying villain and a knave—
Oi took the picture to me mistress ;
An' what o' that, a picture, sir,
Is not a man, so help me Mary
An' all the saints, what's wrong o' that ? ''
'' But thou didst take it to the temple,
And saw'st thy mistress look upon
The face upon the picture ? ''

                    Indade !
An' sure, yer honor, so ye say—
I' faith it is a purty picture.''
Fair Auma, what hast thou to say,
What is thy knowledge of this matter ? ''
'' Most noble judge. I'm pained and grieved
That I should thus be called to answer
This question, that may compromise
The honor of fair Ideala,
My dear, my sweet, beloved friend.
Alas ! her heart is pure and blameless,
Not guilty of one single act
Against the law or inner conscience.
'Tis but the play of circumstance,
That Ideala left the image
With me, and you Coquin obtained it.
More know I not, but that I deem
The whole, a base malicious slander.''

IX.

Now every eye was turned upon
Fair Ideala, when the question
Was put to her by Ageram :
" Hast thou, O daughter of the Mahib,
Heard the grave charges Lord Coquin
Hath made against thee?   Answer ! "
                              " I have,
Most noble Ageram. "
                              " Didst thou,
While yet a queen in Shalah's temple,
Didst look upon the stranger's face,
His image here upon this tablet ? "
" I did, most noble Ageram. "
" And didst thou know 'twas wrong and
    sinful ? "
" I did not, noble Ageram. "
" And hast thou, Ideala, more
To offer in thine own defense ? "
" Not *I*, most noble Ageram. "
Fair Ideala thus had spoken
With dignity that knows no fear ;
With voice born of the truth within ;
With look that did defy the slander ;
With heart that feared no consequence.
Now rose Arrah, the city's chief,
And with impassioned voice commanded
Grant me, O judges, my petition,
Ere ye decide upon this case ;

Grant me a little time, O judges,
Ere ye condemn this noble maid,
Ere ye condemn the Mahib's daughter,
Ere ye condemn a Virgin Queen !
Grant me a little time, O judges,
For I do crave some words of counsel.
I am not here unbid, to argue
On points abstruse and obsolete,
For I'm not skilled in legal lore.
Of what avail can be the questions
Of bygone days long since forgot ;
'Tis dangerous ground to tread upon.
Assume our fathers' ways were perfect,
Why then not blindly follow them ?
Assume they erred, how can we safely
Be guided by their laws and counsel ?
'Tis here the living ye would judge—
Condemn her ! aye, condemn her,
If thus the holy books decree ;
If thus our fathers did of old :
If in your hearts ye are quite certain,
The gods have writ those holy laws ;
If error proof were our fathers—
Or ye, or I, forsooth, as much !
But on the evidence presented,
I cannot hold this maiden guilty:
Nor is there precedent whereby
Ye justly may condemn her.

     Therefore,

Just judges, if this maiden's sinning
Is writ in scrolls of ancient lore,
Damn ye the laws, and save the sinner ;
For she is blameless of intent,
No guilty thought dwells in her bosom—
Though Lord Coquin hath served the state,
Methinks he now doth serve the devil !
Look, honest judges, upon her—
And upon him, who stands accusing
The Mahib's daughter Ideala !
Which one is the transgressor, which
The guilty one ? I ask forsooth.
Consider well the sentence judges,
She is my friend, I will defend her ;
Her virtues and her life count more
Than all the tomes of musty lore.

X.

Old Ageram, the Island's prophet,
With solemn voice commanded peace :
" Hark ye, O Mahib, chiefs and elders !
'Tis writ in holy laws and old—
And laws are stern, and know no persons ;
They are the bulwark of our land;
By wise men made, by our fathers,
The faithful guardians of our people.
And we, believing in the Wise,
The Great, the Just, the Unknown Deity,
Whose symbol is the sacred sun,

Do dedicate within our temple,
Each changing year, with solemn rites,
The purest of all earthly creatures,
A VIRGIN, to our unseen God!
And this, our Virgin Queen, to foster
The purest thoughts within her heart,
Shall see the face of no man living,
While ministering unto our God.
And yet—herself hath here confessed it—
The Mahib's daughter looked upon
The face of man while in the temple;
Wherefore, our sacred laws impose
The penalty of death.
                         Thus I,
Your prophet Ageram, have spoken."

XI.

Now, with a searching look, did Auma
Gaze long into the prophet's face;
And then from one unto the other
Of all the elders and the chiefs;
On neither face was mercy written;
The sentence was unanimous.
Now did she turn to Ideala;
Her calm, her proud, her queenly bearing,
No sign of fear or woe betrayed;
When Auma's heart, with pity melting,
Surrendered all—forfeited all
The selfish thoughts within her bosom:

Her heart, with all a martyr's fire,
Dissolved in pity to her friend.
For there, unmoved, stood Ideala,
Save when she cast a pitying look
Upon her poor heart-broken father,
Who found no words or tears to give
Expression to his crushing sorrow.
An awful stillness fell upon
The whole assembly, when fair Anna
Expression gave to her resolve :
" I too will die with Ideala !
Stern judges, if the laws demand
That she should die, me too condemn,
That I may die with my loved friend ! "

CANTO XI.

I.

" 'Tis well, 'tis well—yet not so well,
For here's the point to be considered,
The unexpected in this case ;
That Auma thus should stand against me,
And like a silly thing, should want
To play the roll of ancient Damon,
Surpasses all my understanding.
The chance is desperate—e'en with one—
What with the other clinging to her !
But I have set my mind to this,
Though hazardous and doubtful business ;
And if there's virtue in my wits,
Now will I have my prize or never ! "
Thus Lord Coquin unto himself,
As he arose that fateful morn.

II.

Oh day of sorrow! oh day of woe !
That, melting every heart with pity,

Did bring upon fair Eidolon
A sorrow never known before.
Though it is told by gray haired sires,
Who from their fathers learned the story,
That once it happened in their lives,
A Virgin Queen was thus found guilty,
But rescued by her faithful lover,
Was borne triumphant through the flood.

III.

The Mahib did refuse all comfort :
Bowed down with grief he sat alone :
"So swift hath fate hurled this deep sorrow,
That yet I scarce believe it true.
My precious child, my own loved daughter,
Have I deserved such cruel fate !
And yet, and yet, my own sweet darling,
Thou art not guilty of this crime ;
Thy heart is yet as pure as ever—
My darling—oh my child—my child !
But hark! she comes, I know her footsteps."
Before her father, like an angel,
E'en as a goddess fair, there stood
Sweet Ideala, sad and thoughtful ;
Behind her faithful Auma stood,
At reverend distance, inly weeping.
"O father ! grieve not at this hour ;
Let all thy manly pride and courage
Uphold thee, as becomes thy station.

Grieve not, O father! for I go
With cheerful steps to meet serenely,
The fate decreed by Om* for me.
Thou know'st I'm guilty of no sinning ;
Yet do our laws demand that I
Should thus atone a seeming error,
And thou wouldst have me do no less.
Therefore, with sense of strict obedience,
I bow before our sacred laws.
I'm come to ask a father's blessing,
And my sweet friend, dear Auma, too ;
Give this, it is the only favor,
The last on earth I ask of thee.
Thou know'st, death has for me no terrors ;
'Tis but the stepping stone beyond.
Dear father, I shall still be near thee,
And wait thy coming in Nirvana.
Yea, more ! couldst thou behold with sorrow
Such friendship, such undying love,
As here, dear father, here before thee,
Is offered by the purest heart,
Upon the altar of devotion,
By Auma, my immortal friend ! ''
"Go daughter, go—ye have my blessings·
I will not think thee lost—no—no—
Nor will be long in following.''

* Sacred word of the Hindoos meaning God.

IV.

Beyond the city, where the shore,
By high and rocky cliffs is bordered,
And where the high tide madly dashes
Its foaming billows 'gainst the cliffs ;
There stands a rock, far out and lonely,
Its grizzly head exposed to view—
A long procession left the city
Upon its way towards these cliffs ;
In silence did they march and slowly,
As if attending some loved dead.
Old Ageram, the chiefs and elders,
Upon the foremost cliff now stand :
While Ideala and sweet Auma,
In bridal robes of purest white,
Before them stand, resigned, expectant.
Now thus the prophet spoke :
                    " Hark ye,
O people, and ye chiefs assembled !
'Tis writ, and thus our laws decree :
By evidence and by confession,
Before our highest tribunal,
Is Ideala here found guilty
Of sacrilege as Virgin Queen.
Therefore upon yon rock conduct her,
Ere yet the surging floods arise ;
Whereas, through man the Queen is fallen,
Therefore, if one here be so bold,
Soon as the rising flood encircles

Her feet upon yon distant rock,
To risk his life and save the maiden
From the engulfing madd'ning sea :
Then as his bride shall he conduct her
Unto his home, and live in peace.
Your prophet, Ageram, hath spoken."
'Mid sorrowing, many tearful friends
Embraced and kissed the maids heroic.
Once more was bosom pressed to bosom,
While quivering lips whispered farewell.
Then 'long a path precipitous,
In silence were the maids conducted
Upon the fateful rock below.

                    V.

Now higher, higher, rose the flood ;
The vast, the dark, the crested waters,
Still rose with seething, surging sound,
The rock submerging, slowing, surely—
But there, behold ! oh pitying sight !
Their arms entwined around each other,
Serenely stand the maiden friends !
Fair Auma lay her head confiding
Upon the bosom of her friend :
While living, dreaming, only, only,
Within the sweet immortal love
Of Ideala's moistened orbs.
Thus did they stand, resigned and calmly,
E'en with a smile beheld the flood

Rise slowly higher, and still higher.
Oh friendship true and pure and holy !
By heaven's angels envied ;
Can such deep love, that fears not death,
Be robbed of its immortal glory ?

VI.

Still higher rose the flood, until
The waters, now the rocks submerging,
Reach threat'ning to the maidens' feet !
When lo, behold ! Lord Coquin plunges
Into the raging flood below.
Another follows, and yet another;
With strong bared arms they stem the tide,
Amid the shouts and wild confusion
Of the excited multitude.
Now do they ride the crested breakers,
And now beneath the flood sink down—
Full many an anxious heart beats faster;
Full many an anxious eye is strained
In watching for the re-appearance
Of head and form from out the deep.

VII.

While yet Lord Coquin and the others,
Did struggle in the waves below,
There rose a shout among the people—
A shout of terror—a shout of joy ;
And the great multitude divided,

And left an open avenue,
Through which with speed of deer came
    flying,
A panting youth with eyes aflame !
The people all in speechless wonder,
With bated breath, beheld the youth;
Who, on the foremost rock now standing,
A moment paused with outstreched hands—
She sees him, yes she sees her hero—
He leaps far out into the sea,
And sinks beneath the flood !

                                But see!
Love conquers e'en the elements.
He rises, and he stems the tide :
He rides heroic o'er the breakers,
And through the crested waves he dives—
Lord Coquin sees his youthful rival,
And with a cry of terror sinks
Beneath the flood to rise no more.
" Behold, the hero ride the breakers !
See how his strong arms stem the tide !"
Thus shouts of joy rose from the people,
And cries of loud encouragement,
At seeing their young hero nearing
The rock whereon the maidens stand.
" He's there! he's safe !" again they
    shouted—
" He stands erect—he's on the rock !"
But see ! but see ! with speechless terror,

The multitude behold a wave,
A monstrous wave come rolling leaward,
And sweep, with unresisting force,
The lovers three into the deep.—

Poor Blos O'Hare, her head inclining
Upon the breast of Maripo,
Wept tears of joy and tears of sorrow;
Tears for her poor sweet mistress' sake,
And tears because she found her lover,
The hero she had mourned as dead,
Her faithful Maripo.

CANTO XII.

–

I.

SONG OF THE INVISIBLES.

" Sweet Isle of Love,
Sweet Isle of Peace,
Where travelers weary
Rest at ease ;
Where shadowy forms
Do come and go,
And whisper softly
Sweet and low ;
Where cares and trials,
Pain and sorrow,
Are forgotten
With the morrow ;
Where visions, gleams
Of fairest scenes,
'Mid slumbers soft
And sweetest dreams,
Rock tired souls
To perfect rest ! "

"Oh, could I forever listen
Unto this music—but 'tis ended,
And all's so still again.
                              Alas !
Meseems I was a dreaming
Some strange, sweet dream; such peace I feel
Within my soul—have I not seen her ?
Ah, in dreams alone, in dreams that leave
Me only empty, blissful longings—
Albeit, meseems, I know she's here,
My only, only Ideala !"
Then slumber closed again his eyes,
While heralds of sweet rest came stealing
In smiles o'er his fair youthful face.
Hush, noiseless came an angel presence,
A fair sweet face, and beauteous form;
Awhile she stands beside her lover,
Benignly looking down on him.
Hush, he awakes; he feels her presence:
He lifts his eyes ; now he arises,
And longing stretches forth his arms :
"My love, my sweetest Ideala.
Why stand so silent—come, oh come !"
Alas, 'twas empty, empty air ;
His arms embraced but empty air.
Again he slept, again she came,
And stood intent her lover watching ;
Again he woke, again he rose,
Again stretched forth his arm appealing :

Then in the sweetest, softest voice,
She spoke these words unto her lover:
"A little while, a little while,
Be thou content, my brother-lover;
Thou art yet weak and faint and weary;
Rest thee awhile, a little while."

III.
CHORUS OF THE INVISIBLES.

"Rest thou, rest thou, oh weary one,
    The time is near at hand;
From darkness unto light shalt thou
     To Tasmins' shores ascend,
     To Tasmins' shores ascend.

"Rest thou, rest thou, oh weary one,
    Thy longings soon will end;
The earthly heart, unsatisfied,
     Still longs unto the end,
     Still hopes and longs unto the end.

"Rest thou, rest thou, oh weary one,
    Rest thou awhile yet here;
Thy love will come, thy soul's Ideal
     Will come from Tasmins' sphere,
     Will come from Tasmins' sphere.

"Will come from where great Israfel *
    His songs Edenic sings,

---

*The angel Israfel who has the sweetest voice of all God's
creatures.—*Koran.*

From where Lethena's crystal flood
   Is fed by nectar springs,
   Is fed by nectar springs.''

Ended the sweetest song that ever
Fell on the ears of Robert Lane.
Entranced, he listened still and listened :
The rapturous notes still seemed to linger
Around about him everywhere.—
When lo! from off a distant star,
A radiant star high in the heavens,
A glowing light shot down and fell
Before the hero's feet it fell !
Now glowing, growing brighter, greater,
It seeming set the air afire ;
And all around him grew chaotic;
His senses deep oblivion seized.
Behold, within the bright aureole,
Great Astarel* stand in his bark,
His godlike face benignly beaming.
As with his wand commanding, he
Subdues and calms the elements !
Again he moves his wand commanding,
When instant rise his servitors,
Placing within the bark their burden,
The deathless shade of Robert Lane :
When Astarel thus to his crew :

---

* Astarel—name for the celestial ferryman.

"I command the windy spheres,
　　I command the rolling sea,
Where the morning star appears,
　　There my dwelling place may be.
As a flame, I come and go,
As a zephyr, sighing low;
　　Where Night and Day, as in a dream,
　　Meet by the Nadir's silent stream."

CHORUS.

We dwell in the wind,
　　We dwell in the deep,
We dwell on the stars
　　That over us sweep—
The pilot is ready,
　　His oarsmen are we,
Ferrying souls
　　O'er the mystic sea.

Astarel :

"Sleep the sleep that knows no dreaming,
　　Brighter shall the morning be;
O'er the tide the lights are gleaming,
　　Beacons from beyond the sea ;
From the realms of Azrael, *
　　In my bark I'll guide thee o'er,
To the realms of Israfel, †
　　To Lethena's vernal shore."

---

*Azrael—The archangel of Death
†Israfel—The sweet singer of Paradise.

CHORUS.

We dwell in the wind,
  We dwell in the deep,
We dwell on the stars
  That over us sweep—
The pilot is ready,
  His oarsmen are we,
Ferrying souls
  O'er the mystic sea.

IV.

CHORUS OF THE INVISIBLES—BEARING AUMA TO THE SHORES OF LAKE LETHENA.

" Tenderly bear her up higher,
On your wings bear her up higher !
    Wake her not from her deep slumber,
    For she is one of our number ;
Yea, and among us the rarest
Spirit, the sweetest, the fairest !
    Bear her up higher,
    Sisters up higher,
And crown her with glory,
Immortal glory.

" Earth-life is fleeting and transient,
All that seems real—evanescent—
    Only the mystical seeming,
    And the soul's longing and dreaming,
And the heart's hoped for Ideal,

Here shall forever be real.
Bear her up higher,
Sisters, up higher,
And crown her with glory
Immortal glory.

Heart that could love so heroic,
Maid that could die as a stoic ;
Friendship that could not be broken,
Faith that gave life as a token;
Beautiful spirit immortal,
Enter Urania's portal !
Awake from thy slumbers,
Lethian slumbers;
Thine shall be Devachan,
Sister, forever !"

Lo, the vapory mists dissolve,
And dawn, celestial dawn is breaking !
Flooding with light, subdued and chaste,
With amber light the glorious sphere !
While sweet seraphic music lingers
Upon the breath of Harmony—
With soul enwrapt the hero listens :

CHORUS OF INVISIBLES.
" Here,
In this sphere,
Where sorrow can never
Or parting dissever

What Love hath united—
From earth-life divided—
Here, lover, behold her,
Thy fair Ideala !
The real was but seeming;
The seeming ideal—
Here heaven's bright gleaming
Around thee is real !
Behold here the mountains,
The valleys, the streams,
In the irised, the golden,
The translucent beams !
Hear the warbling, the singing
Of birds in the trees ;
O'er attarine flowers
The humming of bees !
Here spring never ceases
On the shores of Lethena,
And Love, re-united,
Shall part never more;
For Devachan enter,
Who bathe in the waves,
The crystaline waves of Lethena! "

The tears from down his eyes were streaming ;
When lo ! beside him stands his bride,
His radiant love, his Ideala !
With eyes benign she looks upon him,
While softly, gently, thus she speaks :

" Now have I come, my brother-lover,
To meet thee on these blessed shores,
The sacred shores of Lake Lethena."
Scarce said, a radiant form appeared,
Attended by a group of fair ones,
E ich image most divinely wrought,
Bearing the stamp of godlike beings,
All eager to pay homage to
This rare and radiant maiden.
                              " All hail ! "
In chorus thus these beings sang :

> " Thy journey is ended ;
>   Thou from afar,
> Nirvana's Portals
>   Standing ajar,
> Bid thee to enter,
>   Dwelling for aye
> Here with the blessed
>   Spirits on high.

> " Hail to thee, maiden !
>   Sorrow and Pain,
> Virtue and Faith, shall
>   Devachan gain :
> Hail to thee, maiden,
>   Here on this shore,
> Love re-united
>   Shall part never more ! "

"Behold, my brother, Auma here,
Surrounded by the fairest beings
That dwell upon Lethena's shores !
She's come to join our friendship holy,
That neither parting knows, nor death.
Now dost thou know me, brother-lover—
Now dost thou see with eyes undimmed—
Behold, you world, from whence thou
   camest ! ''
Then, looking down afar through space
From his celestial eminence,
He saw the great world throb beneath him,
With all its cloudy mass of mountains
And seas that know no rest.
            Again,
With mild speech thus the maid discoursed:
'' Time is forever thine and mine—
Ah, verily, my brother-lover,
This blissful realm, vouchsafed to thee,
Doth grant thee surcease from thy sorrows,
Just guerdon of life's many griefs.
Thou hast not hoped nor suffered vainly ;
Thy righteous mind and noble heart,
Thy love, thy faith sincere and true,
Have won for thee this bles't Nirvana.
May Om* in His great mercy grant
The race of man a strong desire
To lay aside their grosser aims,

---

*Hindo name for God.

And learn to bear each other's burdens,
And learn to share each other's woes;
Seeking to reach with purpose noble
Life's high IDEAL vouchsafed to all.

THE END.

FAREWELL!

What deep, what tender pathos lies
   In this sad word farewell !
Where is the heart that has not felt
   The pang of some farewell ?
What other word that brings unto
   The eyes such tears of grief ?
What other word that doth so much
   The heart and soul bereave ?
Affection's ties, alas ! must break,
   And love itself must yield
Unto this word that holds so deep
   A mystery concealed.
Dark Sorrow cries with anguished voice :
   " Farewell, farewell forever ! "
Fair Hope beside her stands and smiles
   And whispers—"Never—never."
Then Love arises in despair,
   Lifts from the dead his eyes,
Looks up to Sorrow, then to Hope,
   And then imploring cries :
" O God, lift from my soul the shroud,
   For I would have more light ;
Which one of these may speak the truth,
   Alas ! which one is right ?

I cannot say farewell forever ;
   No, no, it cannot be ;
Fair Hope, then let me cling to thee,
   For Love would hope forever !"

Farewell !   Thus Ideala would I part
From thee, child of my fancy—of my heart !
Thou who didst ever 'long the toilsome way,
My soul with hope and cheerfulness repay ;
When oft 'mid thoughts of doubt and fear,
   I paused,
Like some lone wand'rer in a desert lost.
Yet will I be content, if others caught
The motive of my tale, the inward thought
That would give shape unto the things
   that seem,
And make more clear the things we some-
   times dream—
And how the constant soul must strive amain
To reach the Ideal it would fondly gain,
Though e'er so far, the patient searcher may
Find happiness along the toilsome way.

   Farewell sweet maid of Éidolon !
   Farewell thou too, heroic son !
      Dwellers for aye
      Beneath the sky
   Of that fair Isle beyond the sea,
   The dreamland of sweet poesy.

Riedern,
  Baden, Germany, 1891.   C. G.

WALLULA.[*]

"I will tell you," said the Pioneer hoary,
With a far away look on his face,
"A strange and a singular story,
A story of Pioneer days.
I reckon t'was back in the forties,
When crossing the plains, a brave band,
The most daring of pioneer parties,
Came in sight of the promising land.

"'Twas then we got lost in the mountains,
Rough, rugged, and dreary, and vast ;
In the pathless wild Cascade mountains,
Where no white man before us had passed.
The forests around us seemed endless,
With no sign of a path or a trail ;
And forlorn did we wander, and hopeless,
Even courage and strength 'gan to fail.

" The moon had her journey completed,
Twice o'er us one dark stormy night,
When around our camp fire seated,
The boys were a pitiful sight.

---

[*] An Indian name of no particular meaning, but derived
undoubtedly from *Wallowah*, formerly a powerful Indian tribe
of the Northwest. *Wallula* here is meant to signify an evil spirit
—a sorceress—an enchantress.

The rain came in torrents down pouring,
And hungry and cold, we sat there,
As around us the storm that was a-roaring,
And our thoughts were a-brooding despair.

" 'Twas my duty to watch until midnight,
And slowly I paced 'round the camp :
For somehow things did not seem just right,
I mistrusted that cunning red scamp.
The blackness of night was appalling,
And time seemed to hang like a doom :
No sound but the rain that was falling,
And the moaning of the wind through the
    gloom.

" It seems that I must have been napping,
When suddenly, rousing, I found
The red-skin (who had been a-rapping
My shoulder) stood fixed to the ground.
In an instant I grabbed him, and shook him,
'You villain,' I hissed in his ear ;
By his throat with my fingers I held him,
But he showed neither terror nor fear.

" Like a totem, he stood at me glaring,
And wildly at me did he gloat,
When his silence no longer forbearing,
I loosened my hold on his throat ;
Then strangely repeating he muttered,
' Wallula, Wallula, Wallula';

Nor fearing my gun as he muttered,
' Wallula, Wallula, Wallula.'

'' Where are my companions? I shouted,
As I leveled my gun at his breast ;
But the savage his arm uplifted,
Only pointed his hand to the West.
Then slowly kept backward retreating,
Still muttering his fateful ' Wallula,'
While ghost-like he glided repeating,
' Wallula, Wallula, Wallula.'

"Where a high rocky cliff stands foreboding,
By its dismal black entrance, stood still
The savage, his hand still upholding—
An omen incarnate of ill.
I saw that the camp was deserted,
My companions were nowhere in sight:
And this the red devil concerted ;
Yet 'twas strange he would show me no fight.

"Did I tell you, young man, I was dreaming;
No, no, for I was wide, wide awake !
When through darkness a light I saw stream-
    ing,
And through the dead silence did break
A melody, wierd as the chanting
Of a voice that is wondrously sweet ;
As my soul heard the music enchanting,
As the red man fell prone at my feet !

"When I saw my companions' faces,
Like pale ghosts in that light appear ;
When I saw through the cavernous mazes,
Grim hosts of quaint beings appear.
Was I dreaming, ha, ha, was I dreaming?
When I saw her wild beauty revealed ;
When I saw those black tresses a-streaming,
That half her wild beauty concealed !

" When I saw those black eyes that were
    shining;
Like luminous stars full at me,
As she sang on a rock, half reclining,
Her wonderful, sweet melody !
Though strange were her words and their
    meaning,
'Twas her soul seemed to speak as she sang;
'Twas a love song she sang, and its meaning
My heart could understand as she sang:—
" 'Where the river flows westward forever,
Where the mountains look down on the sea,
Where the pastures are green there forever,
Where the forests reach unto the sea ;
There dwelt in his wigwam my lover,
Long ago, in the land by the sea,
Where the river flows westward forever,
Where the mountains look down on the sea.

" 'But my lover was false, and I waited
I vain for his coming to me ;

Through the mists of the years have I waited
His coming from the land by the sea.
Where the river flows westward forever,
Where the mountains look down on the sea,
His race shall be gone forever,
Forever from the land by the sea.

" 'When the last of his race forever,
When the last of his race is no more,
Wallula will be silent forever ;
Wallula will lure men no more.
For thee have I waited, false lover,
For thee have I waited alone ;
Till the last of thy race shall forever,
Forever be graven in stone.

"Enchanted I listened, and listened ;
It seemed like a mystical dream—
The cavern around me now glistened;
In colors of a changeful gleam.
While still those black eyes were a-shining
Like luminous stars full at me,
As she sang, on a rock still reclining,
Her wondrously sweet melody.

" Then around in a circle were swinging,
A wierd and fantastical crew,
While to them Wallula was singing,
Commanding the mystical crew—
When up sprang the savage a-crying,

'Wallula, Wallula, Wallula,'
The crew in a chorus replying,
'Wallula, Wallula, Wallula.'

" 'Twas a dismal and fog laden morning,
When I awoke in the the chilly damp air,
And as reason came slowly returning,
Still on me the savage did stare.
But motionless there he was standing,
A sentinel silent and lone ;
A statue in aspect commanding—
A statue forever—of Stone ! ''

YELLEPT.*

The battle is over, the victors are gone,
And the vanquished are left with their dead
  alone.

Alone in the wild, wide plain of the West,
Neath the shadow of Hood's white, towering
  crest.

In a long, silent row, lie the dead of the braves,
Whose kinsmen are mournfully digging
  their graves.

The old chief, with solemn and grief-stricken
  face,
On each painted warrior is turning his gaze.

Now seeming his eagle eyes suddenly found
The object he sought 'mid the dead on the
  ground.

In his sinewy bosom a storm is preparing,
As mutely he stands at a bloody corse star-
  ing.

*Yellept, a noble chief of the Walla Walla Indians of Eastern
Oregon, is described by Lewis & Clarke in their journal as "A
man of much influence not only in his own, but in the neighbor
ing nations. * * We may, indeed, justly affirm that of all the
Indians we have met since leaving the United States, the Wallawallahs were the most hospitable, honest and sincere."

Now he cries to his faithful, his grief-stricken
    band,
"*O tilikum nika,** your chief doth command !

"Go tell ye my people, the warriors and all,
To come and to hasten to Yellept's last call !"

Ere the sun had rolled o'er the great hills to
    the sea,
Were gathered 'round Yellept his people.

                         Spoke he,
Their beloved old chief, as he lifted his eyes,
With the fire of former days, up to the skies:

"O *Italipas,*† witness my warriors are slain,
And swiftly comes death like a wolf o'er the
    plain,

" And snatches my people like sheep from a
    fold,
Like birds they are dying from hunger and
    cold.

" Behold, oh my people, why Yellept doth
    mourn :
Of five noble sons that to me had been born,

" The last one, alas ! by the white man is
    slain ;

Tilikum nika (Chinook jargon)—My people.
†*Italipis* (Chinook jargon),—Deity, supernatural being.

And here 'mid the dead he lies on the
   plain.

"O my people, hath Yellept not cause for his
   grief !
Ingratitude basely hath robbed your old
   chief

"Of his sons, of his home, aye, the soil where
   I stand—
Though I, oh my people, e'en I with this
   hand,

" Gave the white man when hungry my
   *kamas** to eat,
And warmed in my wigwam his cold wan-
   d'ring feet !

"O brave Wallawallahs, your *hyas tyee*,*
I, Yellept, have ever been faithful to ye.

" Why silent, my people, ye are not afraid ?
My counsels ye have and my will e'er obeyed:

" To do as I bid you, I, Yellept your chief.
O *Saghalie tyee*,† thou hearest thy chief !

" To the ghosts of his fathers, old Yellept
   must go,
To my sons, happy hunting ground, Yellept
   must go !

Kamas—Food, a sweet bulbous root.
†*Saghalie tyee*—God, Chief above.

"Bury me, warriors, here on the plain,
Bury me, friends, with the last of the slain !

"Dig the grave, warriors, dig the grave
  deep,
And with his last son, lay your old chief to
  sleep !"

Thus sternly commanded the chief with a
  frown,
And threw on the form of the dead him
  down.

Amid loud lamentations, his people obeyed,
And Yellept, their chieftain, was tenderly
  laid

Alive in his grave, and they buried him
  deep,
With the last of his sons, they buried him
  deep.

Hyas tyee—High chief.

Amoris Memoria.

Night came breathless o'er me stealing,
And with her bright eyes appealing,
And her soft and shadowy arms,
Wrapped my senses in her charms,
As my thoughts passed roaming o'er
Unforgotten days of yore.

But I was not long in musing,
Ere my senses grew confusing ;
On the silent wings of even,
Softly, from the slumb'rous heaven,
Dropped the folds of Psyche's veil,
O'er my spirit weak and frail ;
At the touch, arose a form—
Airy, mystic, beauteous form !

And together we arose
In an Eden of Repose,
Where a sun, eternal, bright,
With its pale and golden light ;
With its opalescent beams,
Shone upon the shores enhanced,
And upon our eyes entranced.

Here in silence did we wander,
And with every footstep wonder

At the fairy birds and flowers,
At the shady groves and bowers,
At the liquid silvery stream,
And the songs of seraphim.

Lo ! there rose before our sight
A graceful tomb of marble-white !
And upon it bright and bold,
Shone these words in burnished gold :
    "AMORIS MEMORIA."

As with longing eyes I gazed,
And the letters' meaning traced,
Saw I melt the marble white
Into form of radiant light—
Form of woman, fair, yet human,
That my arms no longer clasped !

Then I heard, with rapturous ear,
Music of a voice, how dear!
And my soul o'ercame a longing—
Sweet, impassioned, empty longing ;
Alas ! the beauteous vision fled,
And the sweetest voice was dead.

Longing still, stood I, and sighing,
Stretching forth my arms in vain—
Memory only, never dying,
Only—only, did remain.

SUNSET IN OREGON.

A drowsy stillness steals o'er hill and vale ;
And field, and forest, wrapped in smoky haze,
All seem to feel the day's departing grace,
As gentle Even draws her mystic veil
O'er Nature's tired face.
But see ! the lord of day, his golden mail,
Resplendent o'er the western skies displays ;
When all the mountains 'neath his flood of
    rays,
In semi-circle 'round the throbbing main,
Transfigured stand ; a luminous, crimsoned
    crew,
Their rugged brows, in azure-tinctured gold,
Uplifted high, serenely bold ;
Until the regal train sinks out of view,
And lovely Night assumes her starry reign.

MOUNT HOOD.

Behold his glittering brow uplifted high !
Like sail first seen upon the rolling main,
Appears his snowy head above the plain,
Growing in grandeur in your beaming eye,

Clear and distinct against the azure sky,
Beneath him lies outspread, a vast domain,
O'er which, by nature, he seems placed to
    reign.
A vain procession, passing ceaseless by,
Looks up with wondering eye at his bright
    face ;
A moment only seeming in his sight,
They pause, then sink with the approaching
    night,
Into oblivion's tomb, race following race :
But he, despite decay and death, remains
The proud and changeless monarch of the
    plains.

WHITMAN,   WHITTIER,   TENNYSON.

March 26th.   September 7th.   October 6th, 1892.

—

    Weep, O ye muses weep !
For they were ardent sons and true,
And faithful in their love to you,
    Till life did end in sleep,
And day in night ; when, one by one,
Laid by the harp, his labors done,
    Fell into gentle sleep.

    Sleep, gentle singers, sleep :
Though silent lies the harp, unstrung,

The world has heard the songs you sung.
    'Tis sweet to rest and sleep,
When, in the fullness of the years,
The ripened, peaceful end appears
    That longed-for, dreamless sleep.

    Sleep, gentle singers, sleep ;
Your patient lives won for each name.
The glory of immortal fame !
    Sleep, gentle singers, sleep ;
The faith and hope that was in you.
Has taught the world to calmly view
    The end that ends in sleep.

Die Heimkehr.

Sei gegrüßt von weiter Ferne,
Sei gegrüßt du stilles Thal!
Liebes Dörfchen, ach wie gerne
Grüß ich dich doch noch einmal.
Schöne Berge, schaut hernieder
Auf das Dörfchen in dem Thal;
Grüßt den Wand'rer herzlich wieder,
Grüßt ihn Alle noch einmal.

Durch des Lebens Sturm getrieben
In die weite Welt hinaus;
Treu im Geiste doch geblieben
Bist du altes Vaterhaus.
Durch den Kampf und durch das Streben,
Wie ein schönes Traumbild sah ich,
Immer wieder vor mir schweben
Liebe alte Heimath dich.

Kinderjahre unschuldsvolle,
Phantasien süß und rein;
Erste Liebe andachtsvolle,
Schöne Jugendzeit, allein,
Wie ein Talisman erhalten
Tief im Herzen, tief darin,
Blieben alle die Gestalten
Von der Heimath mir im Sinn.

Hat das Herz auch noch gefunden
In der weiten Welt sein Glück,
Sehnt es sich nach bangen Stunden
Nach der Heimath stets zurück. —
Suchend sucht der Mensch vergebens,
Wie beim Irrlicht in der Nacht,
Nach dem Ideal des Lebens
Bis sein Geist vom Wahn erwacht.

www.ingramcontent.com/pod-product-compliance
Lightning Source LLC
Chambersburg PA
CBHW020227030726
47497CB00009B/2981